Calamity at Coombesford Church

Elizabeth Ducie

A Chudleigh Phoenix Publications Book

Cover design: Berni Stevens

Internal illustration: Otis Lea-Weston

ISBN (paperback): 978-1-913020-18-7

ISBN (ebook): 978-1-913020-17-0

Chudleigh Phoenix Publications

For Jenny Benjamin who was taken too soon

St Rumon, Coombesford Parish Church

PROLOGUE
SUNDAY 26TH MARCH 2023

The car park was empty, and the graveyard deserted when Isabella Street ground out her cigarillo on the side of the lychgate and popped the nub end into her coat pocket. She walked back towards the main door of the church, the gravel shifting and crunching under her feet. The congregation had headed off home straight after the service, eager to be in their seats before their favourite evening TV programmes began. Even the vicar had left. Isabella had agreed to lock up tonight.

There'd been a small but enthusiastic crowd for Evensong. Lots of smiles, a few self-conscious giggles, and plenty of vigorous singing. Not always as tuneful as it might be, especially during the psalms. But certainly dynamic. Evenings like this kept her going through the more difficult times. And there were quite a few of those at the moment. Sometimes she wondered why she'd agreed to Henry's project in the first place. So much effort and she wasn't sure it would all be worth it in the end.

She thought back to the previous day, and a very different type of music.

Saturday's rehearsal for *The Hero's Return* had seemed a very long afternoon indeed, especially with all the stupid questions the singers kept asking her. If only they'd bother to read the detailed emails she spent hours crafting, they'd have all their answers. But no, it was much easier to ask good old Bella. Easier for them anyway.

By contrast, playing the organ for today's services had been pure relaxation. She slipped back into the church, leaving the heavy oak doors ajar behind her, and pulled the ring of keys from her pocket. A waft of warm air reminded her she needed to switch off the heating before she left. At least the church boiler was behaving well these days. Yesterday, even Amanda Bosworth had been satisfied with the temperature. Although the visiting soprano had managed to find several other things to criticise instead.

Isabella gathered together her psalter and scores, which she stuffed in her canvas tote bag, still musing on the previous day's rehearsal. It had been a biggie. The first time the chorus and orchestra, all local amateurs, had got together with the professional soloists. It would have been great if she'd managed to get the chorus to put their books down and sing from memory. But somehow she doubted that would ever happen. Hell, getting some of them to look up and follow her direction would be an achievement in itself. And she just hoped Gavin Porter was going to be up for extra practices this week. The young tenor was talented in so many ways – she smiled to herself as she remembered just how talented he could be – but he was really struggling with the first half finale.

Isabella glanced at her watch. Twenty to seven. Time she locked up and got off home. Grabbing the keys, she went through the vestry to the tiny passageway leading to the back door. Isabella knew the chances of the church catching fire were highly unlikely, but she made a point of always unlocking the fire exit – just in case. The downside was that she had to remember to relock it every time. Distantly, she heard a car pull into the car park.

She didn't bother with the lights. The clocks had gone forward last night and the last rays of sunlight filtering through the ancient stained-glass windows gave enough illumination. But as she fumbled with the key, she cursed herself for leaving her glasses on the pew. A shadow flickered in the corner of her eye. What was that? She glanced over her shoulder but could see nothing.

The key finally jolted into place, and, with a sigh of relief, she locked the door. A faint aroma of lemons reached her nose at exactly the same time as she heard a footstep on the stone floor behind her. Isabella turned. Her stomach lurched in panic, but she told herself she was being ridiculous. And coming to the decision which she'd known all along to be the correct one, she walked with a smile on her face to meet the figure standing in the gloom waiting for her.

CHAPTER 1
SATURDAY 18TH MARCH 2023
(EIGHT DAYS EARLIER)

"I can't do it, Edward! I'll freeze, I know I will. I must have been mad to go to the audition. And Isabella must be mad to think I can do it. I'm a good singer, I know I am. But in the chorus! In the choir. Not as a soloist in an opera. What were we thinking?"

Melanie Unwin strode back and forth across the patterned rug in front of the fire. The lounge which took up the whole width of her cottage was so tiny, she covered it in about ten steps – and she'd been pacing backwards and forwards for several minutes now. Edward Jennings was getting quite dizzy just watching her. He reached for her hands, pulled her gently towards the sofa and pushed her into a seated position before placing himself beside her.

"Calm down, darling," he said. "Isabella has faith in you. I have faith in you. You need to have faith in yourself. You know you can do this. It's just nerves. Everyone gets nervous before they go on stage. I still do, even now, after all these years and all those performances. If you weren't nervous, I'd be very worried indeed." He wrapped an arm around her and pulled her towards him, propping his chin

4

on the top of her head and speaking through her blonde bouncy curls. "Let's take a break now. You've been rehearsing all morning and you'll damage your voice if you do too much singing. We'll have some lunch. Then maybe this evening, or tomorrow, we'll go through the whole thing. I'll sing the tenor part and you can practise all your solos. I don't have to leave until late tomorrow evening."

Melanie took a deep breath and smiled up at him. She nodded and pulled herself away. "Okay, you're right. I mustn't strain my voice. I'll go and get lunch sorted out."

"Unless you want to pop over to the café? I've not seen Celia this visit. And I only managed a couple of words with Roger the other morning. Or we could go to The Falls instead?"

Melanie shook her head.

"No, I've got plenty of food in and it'll only go to waste if we eat out all the time." She gave him a cheeky grin. "But you needn't worry. It's all cold stuff. Ham, a slice of Celia's quiche and salad leaves. Even I won't be able to screw that up."

"Don't do yourself down." Edward laughed. "I know you didn't cook much before I first met you. But that Moroccan casserole you produced the other night was wonderful. You've progressed quite a way beyond fried egg and sauté potatoes now."

Melanie threw him a mock curtsy. "Why, thank you, sir. I does me best, I does."

Edward had been under no illusions when he got together with Melanie that he was teaming up with a cordon bleu cook. In fact she was the first to admit she'd existed on ready meals when she'd been living on her own. But for the past few months, ever since she and Edward had been engaged, she'd been taking cookery lessons from her friends. Annie McLeod had shared the secrets of her casseroles and stews at The Falls, while Esther at Steele Farm had been introducing her to the mysteries of baking. She'd even made a birthday cake as a surprise for Edward last time he'd come to stay. So he knew she was trying hard. Now he smiled and nodded at her. "Okay, lunch here in the cottage it is."

"But I've nothing for dessert. So, we could pop over to Cosy Corner for coffee and cake later on, if you fancy it?"

"Sounds perfect."

As the couple munched their way through their lunch a while later, Edward noticed Melanie staring out of the window, biting her lip.

He reached out and covered her hand with his.

"Stop it. Stop thinking about it. You can practise later. Have a break now."

She smiled at him and shook her head.

"It's just so difficult to switch off. I don't know how you manage it. I keep running everything through my head. And then I try to imagine me singing out there on the stage with the whole world to see. And I can't do it!"

Edward tutted, shaking his head.

"Right, let's get a few things straight." He began ticking off on his fingers as he continued speaking. "Firstly, it won't be the whole world watching you. It's a performance in the local church where you sing several times each week, in front of a bunch of your friends who know you, love you, and have heard you sing many times before. Secondly, whatever Henry Whitehead and Isabella Street would have us believe, this is not grand opera. To be frank, it's little more than musical theatre. There's nothing very difficult about any of it. And thirdly, with all due respect to Henry's Great-great-great-uncle Aubrey, I reckon the main problem with this whole affair will be getting anyone interested enough to come and listen." He sighed and smiled gently at Melanie. "I don't want to belittle the efforts of the Coombesford Choral Society, but this really is small beer. You'd be able to do it in your sleep."

Melanie pulled a face and nodded.

"Yes, I know, you're right. I'm just being silly." She paused and twiddled with her earrings, long curled cones that twisted and reflected the light every time she moved her head. "And to be honest, I'm not worried about most of it. There's just that one short passage at the end of the first half. Gavin's struggling with his part and so am I."

"Yes, I did think it sounded like he was having a few problems, although I suspect it's the acting, rather than the singing that's worrying him." He paused. "Here's an idea. Why not have a chat with Isabella and ask her if she could transpose that piece down a couple of semitones? It's only those top notes you're struggling with. And it would probably make it easier for Gavin too."

Melanie looked at him in amazement.

"You're a genius! Why didn't I think of that? I'll talk to Isabella before the next rehearsal. She should be able to make the adjustment quite quickly and that should make things much easier." She stood and grabbed the empty plates. "Right, I'll just pop these in the sink for now and do them later. I hear a piece of Celia's coffee cake calling to me."

CHAPTER 2

Amanda Bosworth flung her score down on the table and crossed her arms under her not inconsiderable breasts.

"This is ridiculous! We're lovers. You're leaving for an unspecified period of time. We're heartbroken! But to look at you, you might be just popping out to the shops for a pint of milk! You didn't even look at me once while you were singing that piece – and it's supposed to be a love song."

"I was trying to concentrate," Gavin Porter protested. "You won't be happy, and neither would Isabella or Mr Whitehead, if I don't get all the notes right, now will you?" He shrugged his shoulders. "It's easy for you, Amanda. You've done this sort of thing loads of times. This is all very new to me. And I don't want to let everyone down." He pulled a face. "Maybe I'm not right for the role. Maybe you'd be better off with someone else."

Isabella bit her lip and looked at the two singers in front of her. Amanda, flushed and irate, like a galleon in full sail, Gavin, pale and frightened. Deep down she knew Amanda was right. But there was no way she could acknowledge that without destroying the young tenor. And she didn't want to risk losing him. *The Hero's Return* wouldn't be the same at all without the beautiful youth in front of her. And neither would she, for that matter.

"Okay, let's take a break, folks. Gavin, be a dear and put the kettle on, will you? I think we could all do with a drink. And maybe a chocolate biscuit." Isabella turned to the soprano as she opened her mouth to argue. "Yes, I know you're trying to keep your weight down, Amanda dear, but you've been working so hard and it's ages since lunch. One little Hobnob won't hurt you." She stared after the young man as he hurried towards the kitchen.

"Isabella, you know…"

"Now look, Amanda." She held up a hand to forestall the torrent of words she knew was about to engulf her. "He's trying his best. This is the first major role young Gavin's sung. I want him to be confident in the words and the music first. He's nearly there with that. And then," she paused and nodded her head, "then we can do some work on his acting skills."

"What acting skills?" screeched Amanda. Isabella put her finger to her lips and frowned. Amanda lowered her voice but carried on in the same urgent tone. "Isabella, he can't act for toffee. That much is evident. I don't know why you gave him the role in the first place. Okay, so he's easy on the eye," she grinned ruefully, "very easy on the eye in fact, I'll give you that. And he's got a good voice. If it wasn't for that final piece in the first half, I'd have no concerns about his singing at all." She gave a deep sigh and threw herself onto the sofa, chewing on one thumbnail. "But he's never going to be a decent actor. And acting is such an important part of a singer's talents if he wants to perform in operas."

"Oh I don't know. After all, I could name several top opera singers who were notoriously wooden on stage, but it never did them any harm."

"Very true, Isabella, but the operative word there is 'top'. They've already proved themselves. They can do no wrong in the eyes of their fans. With all due respect to our young hero, he's nowhere near that league yet."

"But neither is this a worldwide production, Amanda."

Isabella gave a wry smile. "I know people laugh at what I'm trying to do here. And I know Henry Whitehead thinks we're going to make Great-great-great-uncle Aubrey world-famous. But I'm under no illusions. This is a local production of a minor musical composition by an amateur composer." She paused and patted Amanda's arm. "Although I know we're very lucky to have such a professional as yourself involved, my dear."

Amanda opened her mouth, and Isabella wondered whether she was going to acknowledge the compliment or continue with her tirade about the acting abilities or otherwise of her young co-star. But she was never to know, as at that moment, said young co-star wandered back out of the kitchen carrying a tray laden with cafetière, mugs and a plate piled high with chocolate biscuits.

"Oh, that's lovely, Gavin darling." Isabella took the tray from him and plonked it on the table, pushing Amanda's score to one side in the process. "Right, I'll be mother, shall I?" She paused, looking closely at the tray. "You didn't bring my sweeteners?"

Gavin shrugged.

"I couldn't find them. They're not in the usual place."

"Oh no, silly me. I left them on the bedside table after our early morning cuppa. Be a darling and pop up for them, will you? Your legs are much younger than mine." Then turning to Amanda, she picked up the coffee pot. "Black with no sugar, that's right, isn't it, Amanda?"

Once the three had finished their drinks and demolished most of the plate of Hobnobs – and Isabella had said nothing when Amanda reached for her second and then her third biscuit – she picked up her score and adjusted her glasses.

"Okay, my unhappy lovers. Let's try this once more. And, Gavin, I'd like to see you looking into Amanda's eyes this time. You're about to leave her for a long time, possibly for ever. Try to look just a tiny bit heartbroken, dear."

While the rest of the rehearsal had gone well, there'd still been an air of tension reverberating around Isabella's front room. Gavin could feel it radiating off Amanda every time she looked at him. It was a huge relief when Isabella called it a day and escorted Amanda to the door.

"Are you sure you can't stay for supper, Amanda?" he'd heard Isabella ask, and he'd held his breath until he heard the reply, which to his relief was in the negative.

"It's kind of you, Bella, and maybe next time. But I need to get back to The Falls to collect my bag. I'm on the five-thirty train back to Bristol. I've a car picking me up in half an hour."

"Well, have a safe journey and we look forward to seeing you next week."

"Yes, the big rehearsal. It'll be good to meet the chorus at last." There was a pause. "But do try and get Gavin to practise his acting, won't you, Bella?"

"Yes, yes, I'll see to it."

CHAPTER 3

"Hello, Amanda. Fancy seeing you here. On your way home, are you?" Henry Whitehead had just passed through the ticket barrier at Exeter railway station when he spotted the raven-haired singer coming out of the platform café. She smiled at him and kissed him on both cheeks.

"Hello, Henry. Yes, I'm on the next train back to Bristol. I've got a couple of concerts coming up this week. And I need to get a fitting for a costume for that production at the Old Vic in December. But I'll be back in Coombesford on Thursday and will be staying for ten days so we can get the final scenes nailed. And start work with the chorus and orchestra of course."

"Yes, that's going to be exciting isn't it?" Henry cleared his throat and spoke tentatively. "How do you think it's all going? How are the other soloists getting on?"

"Well Melanie Unwin's turning out to be a real star. She's a bit nervous and doesn't realise how good she really is. But Edward – you know she's engaged to Edward Jennings, don't you?" When Henry nodded, she continued. "Well, Edward's working with her, building up her confidence. She's going to be fine."

"And your opposite number? How's he doing?"

"Gavin?" Amanda stopped and sighed, obviously

choosing her words carefully. "Well, I know you and Isabella were delighted when he auditioned for the part. And I must admit, when I heard him singing, I was excited about working with him. But, Henry, I'm afraid he's a bit lacking in the acting department."

"Well not all singers can be a Derek Jacobi or an Ian McKellen."

"True, Henry, very true. But he's not even a tiny part of one of them. To be quite honest, he's more like a plank that's trying to fade into the background." She paused and gave a nervous laugh. "Oh dear, listen to me. That was cruel, even by my standards. I'm sorry, Henry. Please ignore everything I've said. I'm sure young Gavin will be fine on the night. And Isabella's certainly working hard with him. When I left them today, she was giving him a lesson in expressing his emotions. And she tells me she'll keep doing so for as long as she needs to. I guess it's a good job he's lodging with her. It gives them plenty of time to practise his acting skills." She glanced at the digital board above their head. "Goodness, I must fly. I've got to get across to platform 4 and my train's due in five minutes." She stood on tiptoes and kissed his cheek once again. "Don't worry, Henry. I'm sure it'll be fine." And with a wave, she hurried away towards the staircase leading to the other platforms.

"Hmm, I wonder," mused Henry. Amanda Bosworth had sounded anything but certain as she tried to assure him everything was going to be okay. And there was no way he could allow a bad choice of soloist to mar this production. As Henry waited for the train back to Newton Abbot he decided he'd go and see Isabella. If there was a problem, he had to know about it sooner rather than later. And they'd need to come up with a solution. Even if it meant changing horses at this late stage. If young Gavin Porter wasn't suitable for the part of Great-great-great-uncle Aubrey, then he would just have to be replaced.

CHAPTER 4

Gavin had listened to the two women say their goodbyes and the door finally close. At last. He and Isabella were alone. Now maybe they could talk about his concerns, and she'd take them seriously. But as she came back into the room, Isabella was already onto the next thing.

"Right, young Gavin, let's be having you. In the kitchen, please. I need your help with a new recipe I'm trying out."

Gavin sighed as the pair moved towards the kitchen. Isabella was a wonderful cook, and he was really enjoying the meals she'd cooked for him while he was lodging with her, but he knew from experience she wouldn't be willing to talk about anything else while she was in what he called her Nigella mode. He'd tried before to engage her in conversation while they'd prepared supper together, but all she'd talk about was herbs, spices and the wonderful cut of meat she'd bought from Chudleigh Market that day.

So it was much later, as the two sat in front of the fire nursing glasses of wine and pleasantly full of venison casserole, that Gavin finally managed to say what he'd been thinking all day.

"Isabella, I think you might have made a mistake. I don't think I'm right for this part. Although…" he paused, placing a hand on her arm as she opened her mouth to argue, "I'm very, very grateful to you for the opportunity you've given me. I just wonder whether it's too early for me to tackle a leading role like this. Maybe I'd be better off singing one of the minor roles this time around. How about the younger brother, or even the father, complete with grey wig and beard?"

Isabella smiled broadly and shook her head.

"Don't be so silly, Gavin. You're perfectly suited to this role. You're just the right age. You certainly have the looks for the young hero. And apart from that one piece that needs a bit of work, your singing is flawless. It's going to be fine. Trust me."

"But what about my acting? I heard you and Amanda talking while I made coffee this afternoon. You were being very kind, but Amanda is absolutely right. I've no acting skills at all. I'm beginning to think I should abandon the idea of performances altogether and concentrate on recitals. After all, Edward Jennings only does recitals. And he's doing okay for himself."

Isabella nodded her head.

"Yes, certainly Edward has a perfectly successful career as a recital singer, but you could be so much better – and bigger – than him. And being able to perform in a produced opera as opposed to just giving recitals, gives you so much more leeway. I see great things ahead for you, Gavin, and I want to be proud to say, when I see you on television one day, that I had a hand in developing your career."

"But I can't act!" Gavin jumped up and strode backwards and forwards across the room. "As soon as you tell me to produce an emotion, I freeze. My throat dries up and I have enough trouble just singing, without being able to persuade people I'm anguished, or in love, or whatever." He pushed his hands through his hair and exhaled deeply before crashing to a halt on the rug in front of the sofa. To his amazement, Isabella was laughing and clapping her hands. "What? What are you laughing about? This is no laughing matter."

Isabella reached up, caught his hand and pulled him down onto the sofa beside her.

"My dear Gavin, I have everything to laugh about. Do you realise what you just did? You gave me a perfect rendition of the behaviour I would expect from Great-great-great-uncle Aubrey when he realises he must leave his beloved fiancée behind." She patted his knee. "All we need to do is capture that emotion and play that scene out a few times, and you'll be there." She paused and winked cheekily at him. "Right, we've had a long day. Time for an early night, I think. Plenty of time for practising your acting in the morning."

CHAPTER 5

"Esther, how lovely to see you! And Tommy, too. We don't often see you in The Falls." Charlie Jones came out from behind the bar and gathered her young friend and sometime fellow amateur sleuth in a tight bear hug, before shaking her father vigorously by the hand. "What can I get you both? The first one's on the house."

"That's very kind of you, Charlie. I'll have a pint of Jail Ale please. Esther?"

"Lime juice and soda, please, Charlie." Esther Steele glanced down in exasperation at the young collie straining against the leash in her father's hand and trying to run circles around her legs. "Keep still, Tinker!" She looked around the crowded bar. "Is there anywhere we can sit, Charlie? Maybe we can get this stupid pup to settle down."

"Someone's just left that table in the corner. Why don't you grab that one, and I'll bring your drinks over," said Charlie. "So, what brings you out tonight? Not that you're not welcome, of course," she continued, as she placed their glasses on the table.

"We've just taken these two for a long walk across Dartmoor," said Tommy, "not that you'd think it, looking at Tinker, and didn't fancy going back to a cold supper. So we thought we'd pop in here and see what you've got on the menu tonight."

Charlie glanced up at the huge backwards clock over the bar. It was just shy of nine o'clock.

"Well, it's a bit late, so you might not have a full choice, but I'll give Annie a shout. I'm sure she can rustle you up something." She went back behind the bar and opened the door leading to the kitchens. "Annie, can you spare a moment? We've got some special guests just arrived. And they're hungry!"

Annie McLeod came into the bar, her bright pink hair providing a splash of colour in the late winter gloom. Her face lit up when she saw the new arrivals and she ran over to greet them.

"Hello, you two. Great to see you. Did Charlie say you're hungry? What do you fancy?" She glanced at the specials board on the corner of the bar. "I can do you anything other than the duck, that's all gone, I'm afraid."

Within moments, they'd made their choices and she headed back to the kitchen. Charlie made sure there was no-one waiting to be served then strolled over to their corner and leaned down to stroke Frisk's grizzled grey nose.

"He's still going strong, I see," she said. Esther smiled and nodded.

"Oh yes. He's a lot slower than this one," nudging the younger dog with her toe, "and he's not so keen on long distances as he used to be, but for a thirteen-year-old, he's doing fine." She pointed to the bay window behind her. "I see you've got the posters up for *The Hero's Return*. How's it all going? Is Annie getting excited?"

"Oh yes. Well both excited and nervous, really. And of course Melanie's got a small solo part as well. So when the two of them get together, that's the only topic of conversation. They've even got young Suzy talking about costumes and testing them on the words."

"It's called libretto, Charlie," said Annie, striding across the bar with two plates in her hands. "And it's important. We don't want to let Isabella down!" She placed the meals on the table. "There you go. Nothing like fish and chips on a cold evening, is there?" She looked around. "And here's my helper for the evening with the vinegar and stuff."

Esther smiled warmly as Rohan Banerjee placed a basket of condiments on the table. He grinned at her and then shook her father's hand.

"Hello, Mr Steele. Nice to see you again."

"It's Tommy, lad. I told you that before."

Esther suspected Rohan's new business as a private detective was struggling a bit at present. Annie had told her last time they'd chatted by phone that they were giving him as many shifts as possible at The Falls. And Celia and Roger Richardson were doing the same at Cosy Cottage. Now, Rohan nodded at the farmer.

"Okay, Tommy. How have you guys been? I've not seen you since the Christmas party."

"And what a party that was, eh?" Tommy Steele paused and pulled a face. "But it could all have been so different if it hadn't been for the efforts of you three." He looked around at Charlie, Annie, and Rohan. "Without you, I could well have been spending Christmas – and a lot longer – in prison."

"Well, it wasn't just us three," said Rohan. "Your Esther had a fair bit to do with it too. And I don't just mean by keeping us supplied with apple pies and lemon cookies."

"Although, I have to say, they did help quite a bit," chipped in Charlie.

Esther felt herself go bright pink and she reached down to pat the two dogs at her feet, waiting for the heat to subside. When she looked up, Rohan was staring at her, his own face more flushed than usual as well. She gave a little cough.

"Well, I'm not sure how much I really did to help. But it made a nice change to have you guys around the kitchen table for a while – even if the circumstances were not nice at all." The friends had been looking into the disappearance of June Steele – Tommy's wife and Esther's mother, whose body had been discovered twenty-six years after she supposedly walked out on them, hidden in Coombesford graveyard. And in the process, they'd helped the police solve two recent murders as well. Esther, after many years of stress-related panic attacks, was starting to overcome her bouts of agoraphobia, but still found herself on her own in the farmhouse for long periods of the day while her father worked on their farm. She sighed as she tucked into her supper. She certainly didn't want anyone else to get killed, but she did miss those chats around the kitchen table.

CHAPTER 6

The visit to Cosy Café for coffee and cake stretched out until after six o'clock. Whenever Melanie or Edward suggested it was time for them to head back to the cottage, someone else came in whom they'd not seen for a while, or who hadn't had a chance to impart the latest gossip or catch up on the latest news. Finally, Celia and Roger called an end to the gathering and turned the sign on the door to Closed.

"Fancy a quick one in The Falls?" Roger asked. "We're only having salad and cold meats tonight so there's no cooking to do."

Melanie looked at Edward and raised an eyebrow.

"What do you think? We could leave my extra practice until tomorrow."

But Edward shook his head slightly and pointed in the direction of the cottage. Melanie realised he'd been very quiet for the past hour or so. She wondered if he was sickening for something or simply fed up with all the chatter. She smiled at Roger.

"Nice idea, but I think we'll take a rain check if you don't mind. We've already spent far longer in here than we planned and I've a ton of work to do on the score before the next rehearsal."

"Ah yes," sniggered Roger. "Isabella's grand opera.

21

How's it going? I understand we're in for a real treat – or so she was telling us last time she was in here."

"Now don't be mean, Roger," said Celia, flapping a cloth in his direction as she wiped down the tabletops. "You know she's only trying to help old Henry Whitehead out. And I'm looking forward to it. It'll be smashing to have something a bit different to listen to."

"Yes, I know," replied her husband, "but that woman puts on such airs and graces. You'd think she was the next Verdi or Puccini."

"Well, if I don't get more practice done, you'll not be getting a performance at all," said Melanie. She held out her hand to Edward. "Come on, sweetheart, let's get home and you can put me through my musical paces once more."

But when they got back to the cottage, Edward headed for the lounge and threw himself into an armchair. Grabbing the newspaper, he buried his head in it. It didn't look as if Melanie was going to get much help from him tonight. She sat on the piano stool, picked out a few notes on the keys and ran through her warm-up exercises before launching into a full run-through of her part. She was very much aware of Edward's stillness as she sang. He might be staring at the paper, but he didn't turn the pages once. When she finished, he applauded gently.

"There you are, Melanie. I told you there was nothing to worry about."

"Well, it certainly looks as though taking a break from it this afternoon worked. Right," she said, closing the piano lid and jumping to her feet, "do you want to have a quick look at the guest list for the reception? I need to get the invitations ordered soon if the printers are to have them ready in time."

"Not tonight, if you don't mind. I'm whacked. Maybe tomorrow before I head off to the station. Although I'm sure you can make the decisions without me. I trust you." He kissed her on the cheek and headed for the stairs. "I feel like an early night. Don't hurry yourself. I'll see you when you're ready to come up."

Melanie tidied the kitchen, swilling the plates left over from lunch and leaving them to drain. She glanced at the wedding list lying on the sideboard, then shook her head. It could wait until the morning. She made herself a cup of chamomile tea and sat on the sofa, with her legs curled under her, hugging the mug, and staring through the uncurtained windows into the darkness of the garden beyond.

Something was wrong with Edward. She could sense it. He'd been fine when they arrived at Cosy Corner, but since they'd left and returned to the cottage, he'd barely said a word. Was all the chatter too much for him? Surely it hadn't tired him out. He was an internationally renowned singer, feted wherever he went. He must be used to lots of people talking to him, or at him, at the same time.

Slowly, as though it was afraid to express itself, a thought nudged the edge of Melanie's mind. Maybe he wasn't upset by all the chatter. Perhaps he was just bored by it. After all, he was used to a sophisticated audience. Was the chatter in a café in an English village on a Saturday afternoon too parochial for him? A feeling of unease settled on Melanie. That must be it. He'd seen what life was going to be like married to her, spending time with her friends, and he didn't like the prospect. Was he regretting proposing to her? Didn't he want to get married after all? Maybe he was going to call it all off.

But no, that wasn't the Edward she knew and loved. He'd never let her down like that. He was far too kind.

But what if he wanted to call it off, but was too much of a gentleman to do such a thing? She didn't want to trap him into a marriage where neither of them would be happy. If anyone was going to call it off, it would have to be her. She'd say she didn't think she could cope with a marriage where one partner was away travelling around the world half the time. He'd surely understand that. And he'd probably be relieved.

Tears pricked Melanie's eyes as she considered the very real possibility that her dream wedding and happy life with the gentle professional singer was just that – a pipe dream. How could she have been so stupid? How could she possibly think he'd be happy with a simple country girl like her? And there was no way she was going to leave her beloved Devon to live in the city or travel around the world. Living out of a suitcase would be a nightmare.

No, there was nothing for it. She'd have to break it off, give him the opportunity to return to his life of international travel and leave her to her country lifestyle.

But not now, not this weekend. She didn't feel strong enough for that. He was returning to London tomorrow evening. She'd wait until he came back to Devon in a couple of weeks' time. And if she was brave enough – and she knew she must be brave enough – she'd tell him then.

CHAPTER 7

Edward Jennings tried to get comfortable, but somehow the soft mattress wasn't as welcoming as usual. He tried lying on one side. Then he tried the other. Neither felt right. And his head was buzzing way too much for him to get to sleep. He'd not felt like this for a couple of years now. Not since a sudden mysterious illness had temporarily robbed him of his ability to sing – or even remember the music he was supposed to be singing. At the time, he'd thought his career was over. And he'd chafed at his doctor's orders that he take a complete break for at least three months. But if it hadn't been for that enforced holiday, he'd never have come to this little village in Devon, and he wouldn't have met Melanie Unwin. Melanie with her quirky dress sense, eclectic taste in music and an ability to laugh at herself and everyone else, including the up-and-coming opera singer she'd taken under her wing.

He'd watched her today struggling with her tiny solo in *The Hero's Return*. She genuinely didn't realise how good she was. And she was determined to keep practising until she reached perfection. Such a strong personality. And then he'd watched her later, in Cosy Corner, chatting with her friends. So relaxed, her warm laughter rolling above the clamour of voices all vying to be heard. She was completely at home.

He realised, in a flash, exactly what had him so anxious and kept sleep at bay. How could he take her away from all this? She'd lived in Coombesford all her life and had never wanted to leave. Still didn't, in fact. She'd made it quite clear she wouldn't follow him around the world; living out of a suitcase, she'd called it. And he was happy with that. In fact, he'd already decided to cut back on touring and focus more on recording, something he could do anywhere, especially if he built his own recording studio. But they'd looked at all the available properties in the area and nothing was suitable. So they were now widening the search to other parts of the county – or even over the border into Cornwall and Dorset. And with every mile they moved away from the village, the quieter Melanie became. She said all the right things, agreed with his suggestions. But there was less of a sparkle in her eye when they went house-hunting these days.

Edward gave a deep sigh as he listened to the sounds of Melanie shutting up the cottage for the night. Was he doing the right thing? Or was he being selfish? He loved Melanie; had done since the day he first saw her singing in the church choir. And she said she loved him. But was that enough? Or were their lives just too incompatible? He closed his eyes and for the first time ever, pretended to be asleep when she switched out the lamp and slid in beside him. And as he felt her arms slide around him, Edward knew he and Melanie had some talking to do. But not yet. Not until after *The Hero's Return*.

CHAPTER 8

After his chat with Amanda on Saturday evening, Henry Whitehead had spent all day Sunday sounding out the other soloists. And they all had the same comments. Young Gavin Porter was a great singer but no actor. But Isabella had refused to listen to anyone's point of view.

Now, on Monday afternoon, he stood at the gate of Rose Cottage and squared his shoulders, both mentally and physically. He hated any kind of conflict and was not looking forward to the forthcoming discussion one tiny bit. But he needed to have it. There was no way he could stand by and watch this stubborn woman make a fool of him and his family. He'd hung around on the village green until he'd seen Gavin leave. He certainly didn't want him to be a witness to what he was going to say. It would be just too embarrassing for the lad. And the last thing Henry wanted to do was embarrass anyone. But enough was enough. Someone had to say something. And it looked like it would have to be him.

Henry pushed open the gate and winced as the hinge squealed in protest. He hated things not working properly. It would only take a drop of oil to sort it out. Maybe, if the upcoming conversation went well, he'd offer to bring some over later. He doubted if Isabella Street possessed such a thing as an oil can.

"You stay here, old boy," he said, slipping the lead over one of the fence posts and checking that Bertie, his little Jack Russell who went everywhere with him, had some shade to lie in. Then he walked up the path towards the front door.

The squeaking gate must have alerted Isabella to his presence, as the door opened before he could raise his hand to the old-fashioned knocker.

"Henry, what a surprise! I wasn't expecting you this afternoon." She glanced at her watch. "I'm due to go out in about half an hour, but I've got time to put the kettle on if you'd like a quick cup of coffee."

Henry gave a small dry cough.

"Thank you, Isabella, that would be lovely. I just happened to be passing, so I thought I'd drop by and see how things are going on. And to tell you I've had an idea for the final scene."

"Oh yes, and what might that be? I thought we'd settled all the staging. What's your idea?"

"Fireworks!"

He was following her into the kitchen as he spoke, and just stopped himself from bumping into her when she stopped abruptly and spun around to face him, her expression a mixture of disbelief and scorn.

"Fireworks? In the church? I'm not sure the vicar's going to appreciate that, Henry. And wouldn't it break all sorts of health and safety regulations?"

Henry shook his head and laughed.

"Not in the church. I'm not that silly. No, I thought we might make the final scene a sort of pageant with the performers walking down the aisle and the audience following them. And then we could set the fireworks off on the village green. They'd make a wonderful show. You know how much everyone loves fireworks."

Isabella looked as though she was still unable to believe what she was hearing. She turned to the sink and filled the kettle, saying nothing until she'd popped it on the hob and lit the gas. Then she turned back to him and gestured towards the table and chairs in the corner of the room.

"Well, it's an idea, I suppose. It might be a bit taxing for the singers to keep time with the orchestra if they're walking and the musicians are still seated. And it would take a while to get the whole audience outside. But let me think about it. I'll give you my conclusions when we meet at the rehearsal next weekend."

She made the coffee – instant, Henry noted with an inward grimace – and placed a mug in front of him. There was no offer of biscuits, and Isabella had only poured each of them half a mugful. She looked at her watch once again. Henry realised the time for small talk was over.

"Now, Isabella, there's something else I must ask you before I go." He paused and cleared his throat once again. "It is about that young tenor we've got playing the lead."

"Gavin? What about him? He's coming along nicely in the role. I think you're going to be pleased with how he portrays your Great-great-great-uncle Aubrey."

"Well, that's the thing. I understand he's NOT coming along nicely as you put it. In fact I've heard he's terrible in the role. I want you to think about changing him for someone else. Someone who'll fill the role of the hero more appropriately."

Isabella stared at Henry in silence, and he could see she was struggling to find the words to answer him. Maybe she already knew there was a problem? Maybe she was going to agree with him, and everything would be sorted out much more easily than he'd expected? But her next words told him he was wrong.

"More appropriate?" The words came out as a screech and Isabella lowered her voice and adjusted her tone as she went on. "Henry, your Great-great-great-uncle Aubrey was just twenty-eight when he sailed off to the East Indies. That's exactly the same age as Gavin. And he was known for his good looks, according to all the books you lent me.

We couldn't have a more appropriate young man to play the role than Gavin Porter. And he sings like an angel."

"But he can't act! I understand he couldn't find an emotion if his life depended on it."

"Absolute rubbish. Who told you that? Who have you been talking to?" Isabella jumped up, grabbed Henry's mug and poured the rest of his coffee down the sink before putting both mugs in the dishwasher and slamming the door closed. "I'm sorry, Henry, but I must ask you to leave now. I'm being interviewed on Radio Devon this evening and I can't afford to be late. You know how difficult parking in Plymouth can be sometimes."

Henry felt himself being almost lifted from his chair and hurried through the cottage and out of the front door.

"Goodbye, Henry. See you at the weekend." And the door shut firmly in his face. Henry walked down the path, loosened the dog lead, and stood with his hand on the gate. How extraordinary. He knew Isabella had a temper. He'd seen that in her before. But she'd always been reasonable when it came to assessing singers and their abilities. There had to be some reason why she was blinded where this young man was concerned.

"Oh. Oh, goodness me. Surely not!" Henry spoke out loud as a thought occurred to him. A thought so preposterous that initially he was ready to dismiss it out of hand. But it was the only explanation that fitted the facts. Isabella was defending a young performer who was in danger of spoiling the whole production. A beautiful performer who, unlike the rest of the soloists, was not lodging at The Falls but staying in her cottage. "That's it. It has to be!" Isabella Street was having an affair with Gavin Porter. And she was afraid to get rid of him from a role for which he was unsuited because she didn't want to lose her young lover! Henry felt completely out of his depth. He needed to talk to Amanda once more.

***

As Henry walked thoughtfully away from the gate, Isabella watched him from an upstairs window. "Fireworks, Henry? That's what you want, is it? Well I think I can guarantee there'll be fireworks. Oh yes indeed."

CHAPTER 9

As Isabella stood at the top of the steps in front of the radio station, she allowed herself a small swell of pride. That seemed to have gone very well. None of the questions were difficult or awkward. She'd managed to think of something witty to say for most of them; at least the interviewer had laughed at all the right moments. And she'd managed to emphasise her role as the composer without completely cutting Henry Whitehead out of the picture. Okay, so he'd written the libretto and it was his ancestor's anniversary they were celebrating, but without her score, there wouldn't be a performance at all! And she'd got in a couple of plugs about the website and buying tickets. So she didn't think Henry would have much to complain about.

Glancing around, she saw what appeared to be a pile of books on legs walking up the steps towards her. She stood to one side as a middle-aged man with thick greying curls became visible behind the pile. He looked vaguely familiar, and she wondered if she'd seen him presenting the local news bulletins or maybe the weather forecast. As he smiled his thanks, he stopped suddenly.

"Bella? Isabella Street? It *is* you, isn't it?" As he moved towards her, the pile teetered and started to slide. They both attempted to stop the cascade, but it was too late. He dropped his arms and let the final couple of volumes follow the rest to the floor, then put his hand to his mouth, shaking his head slowly. "I can't believe it." Isabella was horrified to see the shine of unshed tears in his eyes.

"I'm really sorry," she began. "Yes, I'm Isabella but I don't remember…" Her voice tailed off as she suddenly realised just who this man was. "Michael? My God, it's Michael Henning! What on earth are you doing here?"

It was more than twenty years since Isabella and Michael had shared a bedsit – and a bed – in Newcastle. He was studying music and just completing his Master's year. She was a second-year English student. Their love of music brought them together, meeting in the University Choral Society during her first term, and their friendship had developed into something much deeper until he'd invited her to move in with him a year later. But by the time she'd graduated, he'd been working in Vienna for a year, and they'd drifted apart. She'd never heard from him since. But then, she'd never looked for him either.

"Here at the radio station? Here in Devon? Or here in England?" She remembered how literally he'd taken all her questions in the past.

"All three, I guess."

"Long story, I'm afraid." He looked at his watch. "Look, I've got to go, I'm on air in a little while, talking about next month's World Book Night. Any chance you could hang about? I'll be done in an hour, and we could grab a coffee and have a real catch-up."

Although she wasn't really sure how she felt about the idea, Isabella couldn't think of any reason to say no. So she helped him pick up his books and sat in the foyer waiting for his broadcast to finish. And during that broadcast, she learned that Michael Henning was not, as she had always believed, a professional musician, but was working in one of the branch libraries in the south of the county.

Once they were settled in the staff canteen with coffee and cookies, Michael took up the story.

"Well, you heard the broadcast, so you know I'm a librarian now. The job in Vienna only lasted about eighteen months. Let's just say the musical director and I didn't see eye to eye on everything. After that, I kicked around Europe for a while, taking short-term contracts but nothing major came along. To be honest, I was a bit disillusioned with the whole classical music industry. So I came home and trained as a librarian. I'm still heavily involved in both singing and conducting, but it was never going to pay the bills. Especially with a family."

"You're married?" Isabella had no idea why that news felt like a disappointment, but it did. Michael shook his head.

"Divorced, I'm afraid. But we have a couple of great kids, so it wasn't all bad. I see them a couple of times a month." He took a sip of coffee and then smiled at her. "And what about you, Isabella? How's life treated you? And what were you doing on the radio?"

They chatted for another half an hour or so catching up on the last two decades. As they parted in the car park, Michael gave her a hug and a quick peck on the cheek.

"This has been a wonderful surprise. I've really enjoyed catching up. We must do it again soon. I'll call you."

As Isabella walked to her car, she wondered if she'd ever hear from Michael again. And whether it would be a good thing or not if she did.

CHAPTER 10

After his abortive conversation with Isabella, Henry rang Amanda.

"Henry, hello, how are you?"

"Fine, Amanda, just fine. How's your week going?"

"Very well. Last night's concert was a sell-out. Tomorrow's looks like being the same. And tonight I am having a rare night off, putting my feet up in front of the telly."

"Okay, well I won't keep you long. I just wanted to ask you opinion on something. It's a bit delicate, I'm afraid."

"That sounds very mysterious, Henry. What is it?"

"Well, I went to see Isabella today. Tried to talk to her about Gavin and whether he's the right person for the role."

"And how did she take it?"

"Not very well at all. To be honest, she blew her top and threw me out."

"Oh dear. That's not good."

"Indeed it isn't. And it got me thinking. And I do hope I am wrong. But it seems like the only explanation..." He tailed off and wondered if he should be having this conversation with another member of the cast.

"Oh do spit it out, Henry. Corrie starts in ten minutes," she said with a teasing laugh.

"Well, I wondered if there was anything going on between Isabella and Gavin. Anything that would cloud her judgment. Make her want to keep him on when he's not fit for the role."

"Anything going on? I'm not sure I understand…oh. Oh, I see what you mean." There was a very long pause and he wondered if she was still there. But then the soprano started talking once more. And there was no mistaking her feelings, even over the phone and without seeing her face. "Of all the selfish, stupid women! You mean to say she's risking your production, the reputation of your family and your ancestor – and my reputation as a professional singer – all for the sake of a bit of rumpy-pumpy?"

"Well, I don't have any proof. It's only a suspicion."

"But I agree with you, it makes perfect sense. It explains everything." She paused, and when she spoke again her voice was calmer and more controlled. "Right, Henry. This is what we're going to do. When I come back to Coombesford we'll get Isabella on her own, sit her down and make her see sense. This ridiculous situation has to be stopped!"

"Well, yes, I've been thinking about that," he said. "You're absolutely right. We have to do something about it. But I've already spoken to Isabella, and she was pretty intransigent on the subject."

"True. She wouldn't budge when I spoke to her either. So what do you suggest we do?"

"We try a different approach. You spend quite a bit of time with the young man, don't you?"

"Yes, I do. In fact, I'm going to be spending much of the coming weekend with him, one way or another."

"Well, I'm sure it wouldn't take much to put a dent in his confidence. You said he was quite unsure of himself last time you were together."

"That's right. Isabella kept insisting he was perfect for the part, and she could overcome the acting problems. He looked less convinced, to be honest."

"There you are then. He's the weakest link. You must make Gavin Porter see he's not the right one for this role. And I'll reinforce the message every time I see him."

"Oh dear, that seems a little cruel. But I guess you're right."

"Of course I am. We can do it gently, show him we have his best interests at heart, but persuade him it wouldn't be good for his career to give a poor performance."

There was a pause and Henry held his breath, hoping he hadn't pushed Amanda too far. After all, there was bound to be a certain degree of loyalty among the singers. But finally she spoke.

"Okay, Henry, I'll do it. And we can compare notes next time we meet."

CHAPTER 11

Michael Henning turned into the church car park, found a space at the end of a row, and turned off the engine. But he didn't open the door. He stared through the windscreen at the old Norman church in front of him. Was he doing the right thing? Bella had seemed pleased to see him last night, but was she just being polite? Would she really want to rekindle their friendship after all this time? They'd both moved on in the past two decades. Although he'd noticed she was reluctant to talk about herself. He'd told her about his marriage and divorce. She'd not shared any details of her own personal life, although he'd got the impression she lived alone.

After their meeting, he'd gone straight home and listened to her interview on catch-up. Isabella Street, former English teacher, now a composer and music teacher, was being interviewed by Pippa Quelch about the upcoming tercentenary of someone called Aubrey Whitehead, and the opera she was writing in celebration of the event. Michael had never heard of the Whitehead family, and it didn't sound like anyone else had either. But it was Isabella he was concentrating on. And Michael had been pulled back many years to evenings spent poring over a keyboard with her, as she helped him work on the composition he was preparing for his final dissertation. He'd decided on the spur of the moment that he would come to Coombesford and talk to her again. Just for old times' sake. And if there was a tiny flame of hope deep inside him that maybe they could become more than friends once more, he wasn't going to analyse that at the moment.

Michael gave himself a mental shake and got out of the car, locking it carefully before heading towards the church. She'd mentioned yesterday that Tuesday was rehearsal night for the choir and as he approached he heard singing accompanied by an electric keyboard. He slipped inside through the half-open door. The singers were in the choir stalls at the front of the church, but the rear of the building was in shadow. He slid into the back pew and settled down to listen, not wanting to interrupt Isabella while she was working. He'd wait until the rehearsal was finished and then move forward. He thought he'd better do it while there were still some of the others around. He didn't want to startle her.

At first, he just let the music wash over him, entranced as always by the variety of ways in which just eight notes could be combined to make such a harmonious sound. And he had to admit it was enchanting. If Isabella had written this, she really was a wonderful composer. Even when they'd been together in Newcastle, he'd wondered why she was concentrating on English rather than music. She'd always said she was happier as a talented amateur rather than trying to make it in the cutthroat world of professional music.

It came to him initially as a slight inkling, a niggle at the back of his head. That phrase sounded familiar. He told himself not to be silly; he was imagining things. After all, there were so many classical pieces out there, not to mention all the popular stuff. It was inevitable there would be an occasional repetition. Or even a nod towards a much-loved piece. Let's face it, several of the biggest names in classical composing had worked on variations of music written by their predecessors. But gradually, the feeling of déjà vu grew. And finally, he could ignore the facts no longer. This music wasn't new to him. He'd heard it before; twenty years before. When Isabella and he had worked together on it. He'd always wondered what had happened to the score for his dissertation piece. And now he knew. It was being passed off as an original piece of writing by a music teacher in Devon, in celebration of the life of a minor luminary no-one had ever heard of.

Michael felt a disappointment growing inside him. He rose and quickly left the church, pulling the heavy oak door closed quietly. When he reached the car, he jumped in, jabbing the key into the ignition. But he didn't switch the engine on. Not yet.

How could she do this? She'd stolen his music and was passing it off as her own. No wonder there had been a certain reticence in her manner last night. Although he didn't mind his music being used. After all, it'd been hidden away for so long and he hadn't even had any idea where it was. But that she would try to pass it off as her own composition. Now that really hurt.

CHAPTER 12

Isabella stared at the score on the table in front of her, chewing her pencil. The changes Melanie had suggested were simple and made a lot of sense. She'd just jot them down on her master copy then transfer them to the Sibelius software and pop them into Dropbox for the musicians to pick up. Although, if she was honest with herself, it wasn't the music causing her a problem at the moment.

There'd been odd moments over the past few months when she'd wondered if she was wrong to keep all the credit for this composition to herself. Maybe it would be better to share the limelight with Michael Henning. But those wobbles hadn't lasted very long. Thinking back to those long-gone days in that little bedsit in Newcastle, she remembered a rather shy diffident young man, older than her in years but lacking in her confidence. In her mind, he might have been the one studying music, but she was the one with all the flair and the ideas. It was she who'd taken his frankly rather pedestrian compositions and encouraged him to add some fire, turning a mediocre dissertation piece into the best one presented by a student that year. Yes, as far as she was concerned this was far more her musical output than Michael's. There was no way she was going to give him joint billing. And she'd had no idea where he was;

until now. Monday's encounter changed things considerably.

Plus she still had a difficult conversation to have with Henry Whitehead. She had to follow the courage of her convictions and some of the narration would need to be changed. And she had to decide how to deal with Henry's outlandish suggestion for a moving tableau ending with fireworks on the village green! She wondered if he'd accept a static closing scene in the church, after which he could invite people outside for one final surprise. Yes, that might just work. She'd talk to him when she saw him at the rehearsal on Saturday. No, that was no good. There was a risk he'd take some persuading and she didn't want the company to see their musical director and their principal sponsor arguing. That wouldn't be good for morale. Not good at all. Instead, she'd invite him around for supper on Friday night. Gavin was going out with some of the singers, so she and Henry could have a quiet meal together. She'd ply him with some decent wine – it would make a nice change from all that local beer he drank in The Falls – and she'd bring him around to her way of thinking.

As she applied herself to transcribing the notes, the land-line rang. She glanced at the display. The number was vaguely familiar, but not one of her friends, as there was no name, just a mobile number.

She stared at the device as it continued to demand her attention. After about eight rings, it stopped, but immediately started again. Perhaps the caller thought they'd dialled the wrong number first time around.

This time, the sound continued until it reached twenty rings. Isabella had it set for the longest possible period so she could reach it from the garden or wherever she happened to be in the cottage. There was a click as the answerphone activated. As soon as she heard the rasping female voice at the other end, she knew who it was.

"Bella, I know you're there. So pick up the damn phone!" There was a pause and a sigh, then the voice continued. "Okay, have it your own way. But I know you're listening. It's far too early for you to be out and about." There was another pause and the sound of her caller taking a drag of a cigarette and coughing noisily, obviously without taking the receiver away from her mouth. "Bella, I need to talk to you urgently. I'll be around to see you at half ten tomorrow morning. And please don't bother trying to avoid me. If you're not in, I'll sit on your doorstep until you come back. And you know I can be just as stubborn as you. Tomorrow, Bella, half ten. See you then." There was a click as the call was abruptly disconnected.

Isabella stared out of the window as the implications of the message sank in. The caller hadn't given her name, but she'd recognise the tobacco-roughened voice of Penelope Conway anywhere. Penny was her landlady. At least, she was her landlady insofar as she was the owner of the cottage, inherited from her late mother, Cynthia. Now she'd been a real lady. Isabella had moved in as her lodger fifteen years before, when Cynthia was still hale and hearty. Despite their age difference, the two women had bonded quickly and when Cynthia was taken ill five years ago, Isabella hadn't thought twice before taking on the role of carer for her friend. At Cynthia's funeral last year, it was Isabella who'd been the chief organiser and mourner.

Two days later, she'd received her first visit from Penny, Cynthia's estranged daughter. And Penny was a very different character from her mother. Isabella wondered what was so urgent this time. Over the past few months, there'd been all sorts of issues raised by Penny. Although she'd been noticeably much quieter when Isabella had asked for a contribution towards the cost of repairing the back fence that had blown down in the winter gales. That had been a different question altogether.

Still, Penny could wait. Isabella picked up her pencil and reapplied herself to the score. She really must get these changes finished today.

CHAPTER 13

Isabella was working in the back garden planting her second batch of broad bean seeds when she heard the front gate squeak. People were always telling her she should get that squeak seen to. That all it would take would be a bit of oil. In fact Henry Whitehead had even offered to do it for her on more than one occasion. But they were all missing the point. It was her early warning system. She couldn't abide people creeping up on her unannounced. And this way she always knew when someone was coming to call.

From her current position, she was unable to see who'd just entered the front garden, but the sound of leather soles on her gravel path gave her a clue. And the dry little cough that came just before her visitor knocked was confirmation. Henry! Henry was back. Probably here to nag her about replacing Gavin again. As if!

She tiptoed across the grass and slipped inside her garden shed, pulling the door closed behind her. There was a tatty old armchair in the corner, covered in a faded tartan picnic blanket and she sank gently into it. At that moment, a shadow passed by the window and knuckles rapped sharply on the door.

"Isabella, are you in there? It's only me."

Grimacing, she pulled herself to her feet. This man knew

her only too well.

"I'm in here, Henry, come on in," she said, grabbing a bag of seeds and a couple of clay pots from the bench. "Just making a start on this year's green peppers." As he pushed his way in through the door, she pinned a welcoming smile on her face. "What a surprise. And so soon after Monday's visit." She tapped him playfully on the arm, inwardly smiling at the faint smudge of seed compost she left behind. "I hope you're not going to nag me about young Gavin again. We had a great rehearsal last night. I really think he's coming along well."

"No, no, Isabella. You'll hear nothing more from me on that subject. I'm happy to leave that all to you." Henry wiped the compost off his jacket sleeve with a fastidious finger. "No, I was just calling in, as I was passing. I wondered if you could let me know your thoughts about that final scene and my suggestion about turning it into a tableau." He rubbed his hands together. "It's going to be such a wonderful climax to the story. Great-great-great-uncle Aubrey returning from the East Indies a rich man and a hero, ready to claim his young bride, only to find she's died while he was away." He stared into the distance, a dreamy look on his face. "I can just see the closing moments, as he gazes to the sky, filled with fireworks, and promises his lost love he'll never marry but will dedicate the rest of his life to her memory." Henry wiped a tear from the corner of his eye. "Sorry, Isabella. I'm just a silly old romantic. The thought of that selfless act gets me every time." He breathed out deeply and cocked his head on one side. "So come on, Isabella, put me out of my misery. What do you think?"

Isabella bit her lip. The fireworks might be okay, but expecting the moving tableau was a step too far for this largely amateur company. And privately, she had her own views on Great-great-great-uncle Aubrey's selfless gesture. She was going to have to come clean at some point. But not now. She smiled at her visitor.

"Okay, Henry, how about you come to supper on Friday

evening? Gavin's going out with Amanda and some of the chorus, so we'll be able to finalise all the details then. How does that sound?"

"It sounds perfect, Isabella. I look forward to it. And I'll bring something special from my cellar so we can celebrate reaching the finishing line together." He clapped his hands together and turned to the door. "Right, I'll leave you to it. Those clouds look like they're thickening to me. Better get your gardening finished before the weather closes in." And tipping his hat to her, he walked away, leaving the door open.

Isabella watched his straight back as he strode away.

"Celebration, is it, Henry? I'm not so sure about that. Not so sure at all."

CHAPTER 14

Isabella and Gavin had just finished eating supper and he'd offered to wash up while she put her feet up and relaxed in the front room. She was just settling in to her favourite soap, a guilty secret she thought no-one else knew about, when the phone rang. That was strange. People rarely rang her on the landline these days, but this was the second call of the day. Maybe Penny had changed her mind and was ringing to cancel their appointment. She turned the sound off on the TV and picked up the receiver. With a strawberry cream in her mouth, her response was slightly muffled.

"Mmm. Hello?"

"Isabella? Isabella, is that you?"

She sat up straight as she recognised the voice at the other end.

"Yes, hello, this is she. Who's this?"

"It's Michael Henning."

"Michael, how lovely to hear from you. And it was wonderful to catch up on Monday evening." She wondered how he'd got her number. She'd been careful not to give it to him at the radio station.

"I listened to your interview, Isabella. On Monday night. You never mentioned *The Hero's Return* when we chatted."

"Didn't I? No, I suppose I didn't. We had so much to

talk about, it never came up."

"The thing is, Isabella, I came to Coombesford, to see you."

"You did? When? Why didn't you come and talk to me?"

"I came during yesterday's rehearsal. I was at the back of the church, listening."

"Oh."

"Yes, oh indeed. I know what you did, Isabella."

Isabella's heart sank as she realised she might be in for a bit of a fight here.

"I'm not sure I like the sound of your tone, Michael. And what precisely is it you think I've done?"

"You stole my music, Isabella. I listened to three of the arias and they're all taken directly from my dissertation piece."

"Rubbish. You're imagining things. How can you possibly think I'd do a thing like that?"

"Because that music is imprinted on my brain, Isabella. I always wondered where the score had disappeared to – and now I know. You stole it. You used it. And you're passing it off as your own."

"Michael, this is complete nonsense. I wrote this opera myself – well, the music anyway. And that's all there is to it. Now I'm going to put the phone down before you say something you regret."

"Isabella, do not put the phone down on me. I know that's my music and I want some recognition for it. I'm not going to stop you from using it – it sounded really good, by the way and some of your singers are superb – but I can't allow you to take full credit for something that was mainly written by me, with just some minor input from you."

"You can't allow? You can't allow?" Isabella was getting really cross now, and it was made worse by the quiet, even tone her caller was managing to put across. "And what pray do you intend to do about it?"

"I'll go to the press. They're sure to be interested in how their great local composer is actually a thief and a plagiarist.

And I'll go to your Mr Henry Whitehead. I'm sure he'd be most unwilling to have any such scandal associated with his precious family."

Isabella gave a laugh, although even she could hear it didn't sound as confident as she might have liked it to be.

"And where's your proof, Michael?"

"Proof? The proof's in the fact that I recognised several of the tunes you've supposedly written."

"But that's not proof, Michael. It's merely hearsay. Where's the score? Where's the written evidence this is your music? Do you have a copy?" Back when they were at Newcastle together, he'd been having problems with his computer, and they'd backed up all his files on her machine for safekeeping. She was pretty certain he didn't have the original. And she knew he didn't have a physical copy, as she'd packed the only one in her luggage when she closed up the flat after he departed for Vienna. She just hoped he didn't remember there was a copy lodged in the university library.

"No, I don't have a copy, Isabella, you know I don't. But it's all in my head, even now, after all these years."

"Well, all I can say is good luck with that, Michael. Without proof to substantiate these ridiculous claims, you don't have a leg to stand on. So, go ahead, do your worst. Go to the press. They say there's no such thing as bad publicity. And a bit of a scandal could be just what we need to build our profile in the weeks leading up to the performance. Because, who's going to believe you, Michael? Who's going to take the word of a washed-up, would-be composer and singer who couldn't hack it on the professional circuit against that of a well-respected local figure and popular music teacher who's just trying to do her bit to put this village and one of its prominent historical figures on the map?" She paused and her fingers strayed to the box of chocolates once more. "As I said, Michael, do your worst. I'll see you in court!" And Isabella slammed down the phone.

"Who was that?" asked Gavin as he walked into the room with a tray of coffee. Isabella gave him smile which she hoped wasn't as shaky as she felt.

"Wrong number," she lied, reaching for the TV remote, and switching the sound back on once more.

CHAPTER 15

Isabella toyed with the idea of calling Penelope Conway's bluff and just going out for the day. She could spend the time in Torquay doing a bit of shopping and have lunch at Pizza Express. But then she remembered Michael Henning saying he lived – and she assumed also worked – in Torquay, so decided that wasn't a good idea. Maybe a day in Exeter instead? She could go in by bus and not come home until early evening. Surely her landlady would have given up and gone home by then?

But in the end, she decided she might as well stay in and listen to what the other woman had to say. Not that she expected it to be anything in particular. There was always some crisis or other where Penelope Conway was concerned – and it usually turned out to be something and nothing. And she doubted if she'd be on time. Maybe she'd not even turn up. One never knew with Penny.

However, she changed her mind when she saw the shambling figure at her gate at precisely ten-thirty. Dressed in her customary black leathers, and leaving her precious motorbike propped against the fence, this was a very different Penny from the one Isabella had first met at Cynthia's house two years ago, or even the one sobbing at the wake. Isabella had been pretty certain she was sobbing over missed opportunities rather than the loss of a mother, but that was another story. Then, she'd been comfortably overweight with a round tummy she'd done nothing to disguise. A daily wild swimmer all her life and a keen gardener, Penny's skin had always been heavily tanned where it wasn't covered in tattoos, but with a healthy outdoor glow rather than any sign of artificial tanning or even leisurely sunbathing.

Now, the weight seemed to be dropping off Penny and her skin carried a yellow tinge. Her long grey-white hair, released from her helmet, hung past her shoulders in a lank stream. Something was definitely not right.

"Penny darling, how lovely to see you. Come on in. Come through to the front room. Sit, sit." Isabella knew she was babbling, but she was trying to take in the change in the other woman without being too obvious about it. "The kettle's just boiled. Can I get you a coffee?"

Penelope shook her head. She pulled a pouch of tobacco from her pocket, but at a warning cough from Isabella, put it away again. She ignored the invitation to sit and wandered around the room, picking up ornaments and books at random and putting them down again. Isabella noticed her glance straying to the whisky decanter on the sideboard. She decided to ignore that. It was far too early in the day to start drinking.

"No coffee thanks, Bella." She gave a rasping cough. "We need to talk. About the cottage. There's going to have to be some changes, I am afraid."

"Goodness, that sounds serious," said Isabella with a nervous laugh. "Well, I'm going to make myself a coffee if you don't mind, and then you can tell me all about it." She hurried to the kitchen and grabbed a mug of instant, pulling a face, but realising she probably didn't have time to make a pot of the real stuff. She'd do that after Penny had gone.

"I must say, Penny, you're looking quite slim. Have you been on a diet?" she said as she returned to the front room and settled herself in a chair. Penny finally stopped meandering and threw herself onto the sofa.

"No, Bella, I've not been on a diet." She sounded as though the words were being pushed through gritted teeth. "Anyway, I want to talk about the rent. I need to put it up. By quite a bit, I'm afraid. You're paying nowhere near the market rate and that's going to have to change."

"But I have an agreement…"

"Yes, I know all about the agreement with my late mother. It was annoying when I first heard about it and it's unsustainable now. I am sorry, Bella, but I need the money."

"You need the money? Why do you need the money?"

"It doesn't matter why," was the sullen response. "I just do."

"Well, I'm sorry, Penny, but you're going to have to find it elsewhere. Your mother's will left the cottage to you, quite rightly as her only daughter, but in recognition of all the caring I did for her – and our long friendship – she said I could stay here for as long as I wanted to. And that the rent should stay at the level I was paying at the time of her death. I think you'll find there's no legal basis on which you can increase my rent."

"Yes, I know that, Bella. But I'm appealing to your better nature." The other woman jumped up and began pacing back and forth. "I'm ill, Bella. It's serious. I need an operation. And if I don't have it, I'll probably be dead within a year or two."

"Well, surely you can have that on the NHS?"

"The NHS? Don't make me laugh. The waiting times are so long, I'll be dead before I even reach the top of the list. No, I have to go privately. And for that I need money. So I'm appealing to you, Bella. Please help me."

"Like you helped your mother when she needed you?"

Penelope looked as though she'd been smacked in the face. Then she nodded.

"You're right, Bella, I don't deserve your consideration, but I'm begging you."

"Well, I'm sorry too, Penny, but I can't afford to pay any

more rent. You're just going to have to find another way to pay for your operation."

There was a long pause and then Penelope shrugged.

"Well, in that case, you leave me with no option, Bella. I'll be putting the cottage on the market. There's nothing in Mother's will to stop me doing that. Someone else can take you on as a tenant. And I think you'll find they'll be less willing to follow the wishes of an old woman who was duped into making such a daft deal."

She turned on her heel and strode to the door. Isabella stared after her in disbelief. By the time she'd snapped out of it and run to the door, Penelope Conway was at the gate.

"I think you'll find this cottage very difficult to sell, Penny. If I have anything to do with it, no buyer is going to touch this place. You're going to get your way on this over my dead body!"

CHAPTER 16

After his unsuccessful conversation with Isabella, Michael Henning had stared at the phone in his hand until finally the high-pitched alarm reminded him to replace the handset in the cradle. Well, that had been a waste of time. He'd managed to keep his tone even and his voice steady, even while Isabella was shouting at him, but inside his disappointment was gradually changing to anger. It was lucky this wasn't his week to have the kids staying with him. The two teenagers had become very adept at picking up on their parents' moods. "Reading the vibes" their thirteen-year-old called it.

And throughout the following day, his fury grew. The worst thing about the phone call was that he knew Isabella was right. He was a failure, at least as far as music was concerned. His big break in Vienna had turned out to be a disaster, and he'd left after picking a fight with the musical director's favourite young singer. A few minor roles on stages in Eastern Europe had followed, but once he realised he was never going to be a major star, the gloss wore off the whole thing and he'd returned to the United Kingdom. He was happy in his role as senior librarian in one of the county's larger branches. His performances with an amateur musical theatre company were always very well received by audiences and fellow cast members. Outwardly he was living a contented successful life. But deep down, he still considered himself a failure. He'd give it all up – well most of it anyway – for the opportunity to be a professional singer or composer.

And now this woman had stolen his music. And it was good music too! He'd realised that even before he'd recognised what she was playing. He mused on the injustice of it all, and as he arrived home from work – to an empty house as usual – his rage finally came to the boil. He strode out of the back door, across the tiny garden strewn with football gear and other evidence of occasional teenage occupants, and through the gate to the lane. Turning right, he began to run, and as he reached the beach he headed for the shoreline, increasing his speed to the maximum.

"The bitch! She's a complete bitch," he yelled to the empty sky as he ran. He could hear a thundering in his head but was unsure whether it was the waves breaking on the beach, the sound of his feet pounding on the wet sand, or just the blood pumping in his ears. Twice, three times he ran the length of the beach and when he could finally keep going no longer, he threw himself to the ground as hot angry tears flowed. All the pain he'd felt in his earlier years. All the disappointment at not becoming the great success he'd expected. It all came back to him. And coupled with the fact that a woman he'd once loved, and who he thought had loved him in return, could betray him in this way, it was all too much. He knew he had to do something. If he didn't, the shame would destroy him. And he wasn't about to let that happen.

Michael pulled himself to his feet. It was starting to go dark. He glanced at his watch. Nearly seven-thirty. Plenty of the evening left. It was time to start his fight back. Isabella Street was not going to get away with this.

He walked slowly back across the sand, up the lane, and into his garden. He realised with a shock he'd left the house completely unlocked and the back door wide open. Thank goodness he lived in such a quiet crime-free area. But it pulled him up short. He'd allowed Isabella Street to get to him. That wasn't going to happen again.

As Michael stripped off his damp, sandy jeans, and tee-shirt; as he showered and dressed in fresh clothes; and as he grabbed the makings of a sandwich from the fridge; all that time, his mind was racing. A plan, that's what he needed. Nothing was achieved without good planning. That was the philosophy he used to great success at work, and he was going to apply the same approach here. A plan of action that would allow him to get the better of Isabella, or at least, persuade her to see his side of things.

After all, he wasn't asking for her to stop using the music. Far from it. He was just asking for her to acknowledge his role in the composition. Hell, he was even willing to let her have top billing. He could see it now. *The Hero's Return*, an opera in three acts with libretto by Henry Whitehead and music by Isabella Street and Michael Henning. Yes, that would do nicely. So now he had the final goal in mind, he just needed a plan for how to get there, a road map, as it were. He'd tried the gentle approach with his phone call. But that hadn't succeeded. Now he'd go in hard. He'd write to Isabella, telling her in no uncertain terms what he thought of her actions and what he was going to do if she didn't agree to his demands.

Michael Henning swallowed the last bite of his sandwich, wiped the grease from his fingers and reached for his laptop. Opening a document, he typed his address in the top left-hand corner and then began: 'Dear Isabella.'

CHAPTER 17

Gavin Porter was alone in the bar of The Falls when Amanda Bosworth arrived on Friday evening. They'd arranged to meet some of the singers from the chorus for a drink and then a few of them would be having supper in the restaurant. Amanda ordered a drink and joined Gavin where he was sitting in the furthest dark corner.

"What are you doing sitting here in the dark, Gavin?" she said after the pair had air-kissed on both cheeks and settled themselves at the table once more. "I thought I'd find you talking rugby with Charlie. After those first couple of matches, you must have great hopes for the Welsh Women this year."

The young tenor shrugged and pulled a face.

"Let's just say I don't feel like talking about sport tonight. I just wanted a quiet drink before everyone arrived. I had something to think through."

"Oh, well in that case, would you like me to leave you on your own? I can always go and chat to Charlie myself." She picked up her drink and prepared to leave the table. But Gavin put his hand on her arm and stopped her.

"No, don't go, Amanda. I'm not getting anywhere with my thoughts anyway. They just keep rolling around and around in my head."

"Is there anything I can do to help?"

He shook his head, then sighed and pulled another face.

"Well, I'm sure you can guess what my problem is. So maybe you can tell me what I should do about it."

Amanda had a very good idea what was worrying the young man and that was in fact why she'd come down from her room so much earlier than they'd previously arranged. If she was right, it was the same thing she wanted to have out with him. But for now, she put an inquisitive look on her face and smiled at him.

"Well, I can certainly try. Why don't you tell your Auntie Amanda all about it?"

Gavin sighed and ran his fingers through his thick curly blue-black hair.

"Well, I know I don't have to tell you I'm struggling with this part, Amanda. It was supposed to be a stepping stone to the big time. My first major role. But it's not working, is it?"

"Well, your singing's wonderful, Gavin, and you certainly look the part. But, I have to admit…" She paused, as though searching for the right words.

"Just say it, Amanda. I heard you talking to Isabella last weekend. And you were right. I can't act! I thought I could play this role, but I don't think I'm ready for it. I need to take some time out and get some acting lessons before I attempt anything as big as this. I should just be sticking to recitals."

Amanda looked at the young man. He was so woebegone, she almost felt very sorry for him. But she was worried that a failure of this production would damage her reputation. And it looked as though the plan she'd hatched with Henry was going to work just fine. She just needed to push Gavin gently in the right direction without him realising what she was doing.

"Well, I have to admit you did seem a little uncomfortable expressing your emotions during the moments of high drama."

"A little uncomfortable! That's putting it mildly. I wake up in a cold sweat in the middle of the night, just thinking about having to pretend I'm deeply in love with you and heartbroken at having to leave you." He smiled sweetly as though to soften his words. "No offence intended, Amanda. You're a wonderful person. But…"

"None taken, Gavin. None taken. You're not my type either." She tapped his arm with one long painted fingernail. "You know, I remember how I was the first time I had to play a suicide scene. My director told me I looked like I was writing my shopping list rather than deciding whether to throw myself off the bell tower or not!"

"So what should I do?"

"Well it's very late in the day to be considering pulling out of a production. But if you're really certain that's the right thing to do, surely you need to get on and do it."

Gavin bit his lip and to her horror, Amanda realised the young man was on the verge of tears. She reached across and took his hand.

"Hey, come on. It is not the end of the world. They'll find another singer. And you can go get yourself some acting lessons. Then the next time an opportunity like this comes along, you'll be ready for it."

Gavin was now shaking his head vigorously.

"No, no, you don't understand. I have no fears over leaving the production. I know it's the right thing to do." He buried his face in his hands and his words came out as a muffled wail. "But she won't let me."

"She? Who's she? Oh." The penny suddenly dropped. "Isabella. You've told her you want to leave, haven't you? What did she say?"

"She said she wasn't going to let me walk away from the production – or from her." He looked at Amanda once more. "You see, Isabella and I…" His voice broke. "Amanda, I've been such a fool!"

Amanda realised this was not the time to pretend surprise at the admission the young man had just made. And he probably wouldn't notice if she did, given the state he was in.

"Oh. I see. And what can she do to stop you?"

"She threatened to alert the main sponsor. She says they'll ask for all the money back. All the fees they've paid me so far. And I don't have any of it left. Isabella likes presents, you see. Her little surprises, she calls them. And we've been out for dinner in Exeter a few times. So there's nothing left." He paused. "And she threatened to make sure I'd never work again. She reckons she's got contacts throughout the music world."

"Well, I very much doubt that, to be honest. When all's said and done, Isabella's only an amateur. I've got far more influence in the music world than she has. And I wouldn't worry about the money thing either. Henry Whitehead holds the purse-strings. In fact, I shouldn't really be telling you this, but he's secretly the main sponsor for the production, and I'm sure he wouldn't allow Isabella's personal feelings to get in the way of what I know he believes is the best approach for this production." Gavin looked at her in surprise. "Yes, I have to admit, Henry and I have been talking about this whole sorry situation. So let me have a chat with him and see what he suggests."

"Thank you, Amanda. I've been so stupid."

"Look, Gavin," she said as she smiled and patted his arm, "you're not the first young star who's been inveigled into a bedroom situation by a musical director, and you certainly won't be the last. We can sort this out."

"Well, I certainly hope so." He gave her a watery smile. "To be honest, I was getting so desperate, I was even thinking of knocking her over the head one dark night. I just couldn't think of any other way out of this situation."

61

CHAPTER 18

On Saturday afternoon, Isabella had arranged a full rehearsal of *The Hero's Return*, putting together the soloists, the chorus, and the orchestra for the first time. Melanie was restless all day and arrived at the church well before the rehearsal was due to start. She thought she'd take the opportunity to sort out the music used by the church choir. She'd noticed at Evensong last weekend that it was all muddled up. They were supposed to keep all the copies separated for ease of use, but at the end of the service, some people just threw their music back in the box, in a hurry to get off to The Falls for a post-singing drink.

She let herself into the vestry and settled down on the floor, pulling the box towards her. Pretty soon she was surrounded by sheets of music, so absorbed in what she was doing she didn't realise anyone else had arrived until she heard voices in the choir stalls on the other side of the rood screen.

"No sign of our illustrious leader then? She's usually here early."

"No, we seem to be the first."

It was two of the sopranos. Melanie had never got on well with them; they were known to be the worst gossips around. She decided to stay put until some of the others arrived. But now she knew they were there, she found it impossible to ignore their conversation.

"Mind you, I wouldn't be surprised if she was a bit distracted at the moment."

"Why. What's happened?"

"Haven't you heard? She's developed quite a soft spot for a certain tenor. A really soft spot, if you know what I mean."

There was a cackle of laughter from the speaker, as Melanie's blood froze, and she found herself holding her breath.

"No. Don't be daft. He wouldn't be interested in her."

"I'm only telling you what I've heard. It seems Isabella has been spending quite a bit of time working on his repertoire."

"Well, you do surprise me. Punching above her weight, I would have thought. Not to mention the age difference."

"Oh, there's no accounting for taste. And some men prefer the older woman. More mature. More experienced." There was more laughter, then the sound of footsteps. "Ssh. Here she comes. Better stop talking about her. But just keep your eyes open. The signs are all there if you look for them."

"Hello, ladies, nice and early I see. Are you the only ones here?"

Melanie recognised the voice of their musical director, and just possibly, the reason Edward had been so strange last Sunday. Maybe he wasn't bored with her and village life, as she'd suspected. Maybe he was actually enjoying village life very much indeed – just not with her. That would explain a lot.

But surely not. Edward wouldn't be interested in someone like Isabella. Would he? Melanie was so confused now. She had no idea what to believe. She'd known last weekend there was something wrong with their relationship and if she didn't sort it out, the chances of a happy marriage were very slim indeed.

Melanie pulled the piles of music together, slipped them

into the appropriate folders and stacked them neatly in the box, which she pushed back into the cupboard. From the sound of it, the rest of the chorus had now arrived. There was quite a crowd out there. She slipped out of the vestry and around the rood screen, melting into the group of altos standing waiting for instructions from Isabella. 'Keep your eyes open', one of the gossips had said. Yes, she was certainly going to do that. If Edward had fallen for someone else, she'd be able to spot the signs, she was sure of it. And if it was true, her resolution that she'd break it off was firmer than ever. One thing she was sure of. There was no way Edward, or any other man for that matter, was going to jilt her and make her the laughing stock of the village. No, if there was any breaking up to do then she was going to be the one to do it.

But as Melanie took her place in the chorus and opened the score of *The Hero's Return*, she heaved a heavy sigh. She might pretend to others that she was the strong one who wouldn't put up with any nonsense, but deep down inside she knew she was just a little girl who felt alone in the world and needed some help. Maybe she needed to talk to someone about her fears and concerns. Someone who'd have a clearer view on the situation. Someone with lots of experience in dealing with knotty problems. And this was very knotty indeed.

CHAPTER 19

"Goodnight. See you next week." Melanie waved to a couple of other choristers as she hurried through the lych gate and turned right, heading towards her cottage. She was looking forward to getting home and shutting out the world. Ever since she'd listened to the two sopranos gossiping yesterday afternoon, she'd been able to think of nothing else. Was Edward cheating on her with Isabella? Could that be the reason he'd been so quiet the previous weekend? He'd been wonderfully helpful when she'd been practising her solo for *The Hero's Return* but when they came back from the afternoon in Cosy Cottage, something had changed. He'd been unwilling to discuss their wedding plans and since he'd returned to London, she'd barely heard from him apart from the odd text message. Yes, she knew he had a busy week rehearsing and performing, but even so. There was something not right. She needed to find out what it was.

A figure loomed out of the darkness, and she ran straight into them, bouncing off and stumbling backwards into the hedge.

"Melanie! I'm so sorry. Did I hurt you?" The voice was instantly recognisable, and she gave a laugh as she picked herself out of the undergrowth. It was Gavin Porter, the young professional singer staying in the village.

"No, Gavin, I'm fine. I was daydreaming and didn't see you there. What are you doing skulking around outside the church?"

Gavin had reached out an arm to steady her, but now he quickly removed it.

"Not skulking, Melanie. Just waiting for someone. Is Evensong finished?"

"Yes; just. Do you want to see Isabella? She's still in the church, talking to Rosemary, I think."

But the young man shook his head.

"No, I'm not looking for Isabella. Why should I be?"

"No reason, I guess. I just thought…"

"Look, Melanie, sorry, I have to go." And brushing past her, he hurried off in the direction of the village green. As Melanie turned to watch him, the late evening sun shone straight into her eyes, and she was temporarily blinded. Blinking and shifting position, she was surprised to see that the young man had disappeared.

"How very mysterious. I thought you said you were meeting someone, Gavin. Now, where did you disappear to, I wonder?" But as Melanie resumed her journey home, her own concerns resurfaced, and she forgot all about her brief encounter.

CHAPTER 20

"Isabella, can I leave you to lock up? The kids are going out and I need to see them before they go." Rosemary Leafield made Isabella jump when she suddenly appeared around the side of the organ.

"What? Oh, sorry, Ros, I was miles away." Isabella hadn't heard her friend approaching. "Yes, yes, you get off. I've got a bit more to do here and then I'll be gone too. Great service by the way. I loved the message in the sermon."

"Thanks. Just a pity so few people heard it." She shrugged. "Right, you've got your key?"

Isabella reached into her tote bag and pulled out a bunch of keys, pointing to the ornate black one that was so much bigger than all the rest. Then she watched with a smile as Rosemary hurried down the aisle and out of the front door. She had a pretty good idea that the real reason for her rapid departure was more to do with the starting time of the latest David Attenborough wildlife special than a desire to see her kids, but it didn't do to accuse the vicar of lying, especially on a Sunday.

But Isabella's smile faded as she returned to the problem she'd been mulling over throughout Evensong and for some time before that. Ever since Michael Henning's phone call, to be precise. When she'd started work on *The Hero's Return*, she'd not heard from her former lover for nearly twenty years. And she'd put so much work into his dissertation piece that she'd had no compunction about claiming it as her own. That was why she'd reacted as she had to his call the other night. How dare he reappear after all this time and make demands on her? But now she'd calmed down, she was starting to have second thoughts. Especially after listening to this evening's sermon.

Isabella looked around the empty church. Everyone had been in such a hurry to disappear. Not only Rosemary but the congregation, so tiny it was almost outnumbered by the choir. And the building suddenly felt threatening, even with all the lights on. Not the comforting place she usually found it. But she needed to check everything carefully before she locked up. Maybe she'd just have a quick smoke first, steady her nerves. Isabella had been trying to give up for a long time and hadn't smoked in the cottage since Gavin came to stay. But sometimes she couldn't resist the urge. Grabbing her pack of cigarillos and lighter, she slipped out through the front door and into the darkening churchyard.

Like the church, it was deserted. She lit up, blew out a long trail of fragrant smoke and strolled along the path. Leaning on the lych gate, she gazed out over the village green. The school opposite was in darkness. At Cosy Cottage, blinds were drawn on the ground floor windows but from the apartment above, lights shone out. Celia and Roger Richardson were presumably settling down to a quiet evening before another busy week. Such a peaceful scene. Isabella gave a deep sigh. Life was really too short for arguments. And there were too many problems in her life already. She resolved to phone Michael Henning the next day and come to an agreement with him. She didn't think he had an issue with his music being used. Hopefully he would accept joint credit. And once that was out of the way, she could deal with her other concerns: Penny and the cottage; Gavin and his self-confidence. And Henry. She'd hoped Friday's supper would smooth out the issues there. But somehow she didn't think it had.

CHAPTER 21

Melanie Unwin stopped on the path leading up to the church. What on earth was she thinking? Why did she imagine the vicar was going to be in the least bit interested in her problems? Especially on a Monday, traditionally her day off. Yes, the Reverend Rosemary Leafield was expecting to take the service when they got married in August. Yes, she'd been very welcoming when Edward had first attended services in St Rumon's, and come at Melanie's invitation to the Free Choir on Sunday evenings. And yes, she and her husband had been guests in the cottage for occasional Mah Jong nights over the past couple of years. But Melanie was not convinced her friend and pastor would be able to understand the anxieties she was feeling at the moment. She wasn't even sure she understood them herself.

It wasn't as though Edward had said anything to give her cause to think he was having second thoughts. Had he? He was just a bit quiet these days. Probably concerned about the upcoming tour scheduled for Austria and Czechia in July. He always got distracted when he was about to start performing again. He'd never forgotten the terrible time in London when his voice and his music had deserted him. Although Melanie had much to thank that incident for. If it hadn't been for that, she'd never have met the world-famous tenor who was due to become her husband very soon. And as for the gossip she'd heard passing between the sopranos on Saturday afternoon, she must have been mistaken. Edward and Isabella? What a ridiculous notion. Melanie sighed. She knew she was being silly. But she really, really needed someone else to confirm that. To tell her to stop worrying and look forward to the upcoming nuptials. Normally she'd have spoken to Charlie or Annie – especially Annie – but they'd taken a very rare couple of days away to visit friends in London, leaving Rohan Banerjee running The Falls. And Rohan, nice as he was, was not the sort she would seek relationship advice from.

No, the vicar was her best bet right now. She squared her shoulders, took a deep breath, and marched forwards towards the front door of the church. That was strange. The door was closed. Melanie knew Rosemary was meticulous about keeping the church open throughout the daylight hours, believing it should be a welcoming space, whether people wanted to pray or just sit quietly in the cool or the warm, depending on the time of year. It was usually Rosemary herself who opened the church, although sometimes her husband, Joel, did it for her. Melanie glanced across the graves and the wall, towards the large Victorian vicarage next door. All the curtains were open, so it wasn't a case of the vicar and her family sleeping in. Still, it was very early. Barely seven-thirty. No doubt one of them would be along in a moment. Hopefully it would be Rosemary and she could have her chat while they both went around opening everything up.

Melanie gave the large metal ring a twist, more in hope than expectation, and was surprised to find the door wasn't locked. Maybe it had swung closed of its own accord. She pushed the heavy door inwards and slipped inside. There were no lights on, and deep shadows clung to the walls and pooled around the edges of the pews. Melanie clicked on the lights, flooding the building with brilliance, but not disturbing the silence one bit. How strange. There was no-one here. Surely the church hadn't been left unlocked all night? Isabella had said she'd do it last night after Evensong.

She walked up the aisle, stepping gently, afraid for some reason she couldn't explain to disturb the quiet. The door to the vestry was also unlocked but closed shut. Pushing it open, she groped for the light switch in the corner. Her fingers connected with it and she pushed but nothing happened. Drat, the bulb must have gone again. She must remember to mention that to Joel. He was not only the vicar's husband but also the unofficial caretaker for the building. Certainly he was the first port of call for broken light bulbs and the like.

Melanie knew there was another light in the tiny vestibule at the back of the room. She would switch that one on, giving at least some light for whoever came to get anything from this room. Then she would go over to the vicarage and find out if everything was okay.

As Melanie crossed the vestry, she was aware of a faint odour. Metallic, slightly familiar, definitely unpleasant. She had no idea what it was but knew she didn't like it. The hairs on her neck rose and she wondered briefly if she should just leave now and go to find Rosemary in her home.

She didn't see the bundle in the corner until she tripped over it, pitching herself headlong to the floor. What on earth was that? She groaned, pulling herself to her feet and rubbing her knees and elbow which she'd banged in the fall. And urgh, her hands were all wet. Someone had left this place in a real mess. She reached across to the light switch and then turned to look at what had caused her to fall. By the time her brain registered what she was looking at, Melanie Unwin had already started to scream.

CHAPTER 22

Melanie shivered as she sat on the bench outside the church, gazing at the blood on her hands and smeared across her tee-shirt and leggings. Her mind churned. Who would want to kill Isabella? And why here? Why in the church of all places? She tried to blot out the sight of her choir mistress and friend lying in the vestry in a pool of blood. And she wished Edward was here. He'd know what to do. But Edward was back in London preparing for a major concert later that week and the last thing she wanted to do was disrupt his career in any way.

But then a terrible thought struck her as she remembered why she'd been coming to the church, anyway, looking for advice from the vicar. If the gossips were right – and she really hoped they weren't – Edward was involved with Isabella. He'd be so upset at the news. And although it would break her heart, she'd end their engagement if it was true. She wouldn't want to see him again if he'd cheated on her. Melanie gave a sob and squeezed her eyes tightly shut. She wasn't sure she could bear it if that happened.

The sound of sirens approaching from the Exeter direction pulled her out of her reverie. A police car turned into the car park, followed by an ambulance. A young police officer and a couple of paramedics walked across the graveyard and stopped in front of her.

"Ms Unwin?" asked the policeman, a constable who looked as if he should still be in the sixth form. He stooped down so his face was level with hers. "You made the emergency call? You found a body?"

Melanie nodded and pointed towards the church.

"In the vestry, at the back of the building, to the right of the altar," she whispered. Then she looked up in horror. "You don't need me to come with you, do you? I don't want to see her again."

"No, Ms Unwin, you're fine right here." He nodded at the paramedics, who continued up the path and through the front door of the church.

But at that moment, a tall stout figure in jeans and a faded Guns 'N' Roses tee-shirt ran across the grass.

"Melanie darling, what on earth's going on? Are you hurt?"

The policeman stood.

"And you are, madam?"

"I'm Rosemary Leafield, Vicar of Coombesford. This is my church. And I need to know what's going on!"

"My apologies, Reverend." Melanie thought the young man was going to salute, he looked so abashed. "I'm new to this beat and we've not met yet." Rosemary waved his apologies aside and he continued: "Ms Unwin called the emergency services and reported finding a body in the church. The ambulance men have just gone in. And I'm about to join them. Can you stay here with Ms Unwin for a while? I'll need to talk to her once we've established the situation in there." He paused and looked down at Melanie once more. "Just one question, Ms Unwin. Did you recognise the person?"

Melanie nodded and twisted her hankie in her hands.

"Yes," she whispered. "It's Isabella. Isabella Street."

Rosemary gasped.

"My God, how terrible."

"You know this Isabella Street, then, Reverend

Leafield?"

"Yes, of course I do. She's the organist and runs the choir. What on earth's happened to her? Did she have a heart attack?" But then, looking at Melanie more closely, as though noticing the blood for the first time, she went very quiet.

"That's what we're going to find out, Vicar. Please wait here, ladies."

Within a short period of time, the paramedics came back out of the church, shaking their heads gently towards Melanie and Rosemary before climbing into their ambulance and driving away. Melanie had calmed down, but still felt unable to say anything. The young constable joined them once more.

"Ms Unwin, is it okay to call you Melanie?" She nodded and he continued. "Melanie, it looks like Ms Street's death is suspicious. I'm going to call it in and when someone from the Major Crime Investigation Team arrives, you'll need to take us through what happened here this morning."

Melanie opened her mouth, but no sound came out. She suddenly found herself unable to speak.

Rosemary stood up and put her hand on Melanie's shoulder.

"Okay, constable, I think we should leave this until later, don't you. Can't you see poor Melanie's in shock? The poor girl can barely talk. And she needs to get changed. Look at her!"

The policeman nodded his head.

"Alright, Vicar. Can you take her back to the vicarage for now? I need to secure the crime scene and wait for the detectives to arrive. I'll come over and collect her clothes later."

Melanie heard his words and stood up suddenly.

"Take my clothes? Why?"

"Because they're covered with blood, Melanie. Blood which I can only assume has come from the crime scene. A crime scene you may have contaminated."

"It's not my fault. It was dark. I didn't see Isabella until I fell over her. Literally. And I landed in the pool of blood." Her voice faded to nothing, and she started shivering again. Rosemary took her gently by the arm and started pulling her towards the vicarage.

"Come on, sweetie. Let's get you changed." She looked down at her own statuesque body. "I don't think anything of mine is going to be suitable, but we'll raid the girls' bedroom. One of them will be sure to have something to fit you." As she led Melanie away, she stopped and turned back to the young police constable. "Officer, you referred to my vestry as 'the crime scene'. What makes you so sure this wasn't some sort of tragic accident?"

"Because, Reverend Leafield, I don't see how Ms Isabella Street could possibly have caused her own injuries. So I'm afraid this is a suspicious death, and your church is definitely a crime scene. No-one will be allowed in until it's been forensically examined."

CHAPTER 23

As Melanie reached the foot of the outside staircase leading up to the main rooms of The Folly, she bumped into Annie McLeod coming down.

"Melanie, sweetie. What on earth are you doing here?"

"It's Tuesday, Annie. I always look after Suzy on Tuesdays."

"But after what happened. After finding Isabella… We assumed you'd want a night off."

Melanie shook her head.

"No, really, I'd rather be here. I don't want to sit in the cottage on my own."

Melanie only realised she was crying when Annie flew down the rest of the stairs and pulled her into a tight hug.

"Hush, darling, don't cry. Here, sit on the steps with me."

Melanie sobbed into Annie's shoulder for a few minutes, then wiped her eyes, sniffed and sat up straight.

"I'm sorry, Annie, I don't know where that came from. It must be the strain of the last few days."

"Well it's only to be expected that you'd be upset. Finding poor dear Isabella's body like that must have been a terrible shock."

"Do you think I'm going to upset Suzy? Would you

rather I went home?"

"No, of course not. If you're happy to be here, we're happy to see you. Suzy's always delighted to see her favourite babysitter. I have to warn you, she's in a talkative mood this evening, so I'm not sure how much reading you're going to get done." She nodded to the book Melanie had poking out of the brightly coloured tote bag hanging from her shoulder. "Mind you, she told me off the other day for referring to you guys as babysitters at all. Pointed out she's nearly eleven and will be heading off to Torquay on her own for school from the autumn."

Melanie smiled at her friend.

"Yes, she's right. We need to find another word for what we do. Maybe companion would be better."

"Or even just 'friend'? After all, that's what you guys are."

"But since you pay us so generously for the pleasure of sitting with your daughter when you're on duty, maybe we should be friends with benefits." Melanie stopped suddenly, realising what she'd said, and flushed deeply.

Annie let out a peal of laughter and pushed her bright pink fringe out of her eyes.

"Oh, no I don't think that works at all, do you? Although I must tell Charlie. She'll love it." Then she stopped laughing and pulled a face. "But seriously, Melanie, we'll probably have to reconsider this arrangement once we get past the summer. Suzy really will be old enough to stay on her own in the evenings, ancient though that makes me seem, and once you're married, you won't want to be committed to so many evenings away from home. Especially not once you get your nice new place. How's the house hunting going along, by the way?"

"Er, okay, I think. We've seen a few really nice properties and think we've narrowed it down to one or two. It really comes down to which one Edward feels will be better for him to build his recording studio."

Annie looked perplexed.

"But which do you want, Melanie? It'll be your home too. In fact you'll be spending far more time there than Edward, while he's touring, so it has to be right for you too."

"Yes, I know, Annie, but to be quite honest, I'll be happy anywhere, so long as I'm still close enough to my friends in Coombesford, of course." She stopped and stared over the beer garden towards the distant Haldon Hills. "Although at the moment, I'm not sure about anything. I don't even know whether we'll be getting married this autumn at all."

"Melanie, what on earth are you talking about? Of course you'll be getting married. What's the matter? Are you having wedding jitters? It's perfectly natural, you know, but there's nothing to worry about. Anyone who knows you guys can see you're besotted with each other."

"Well, for a start, I could be in prison for murder by then. I don't think Edward would want to marry a convicted felon, would he?"

"What? Surely the police don't seriously think you had anything to do with Isabella's death, do they? After all, you were the one who found her and called them in the first place."

"Yes, and when they arrived, I was sitting in the churchyard covered in her blood. Not a good look, I can assure you. And apparently it's quite a common ploy for killers to pretend to find their victim's body. A good way to put the police off the scent, so I've heard."

"Oh, Melanie, come on, this is ridiculous. You can't really think the police are going down that road, can you?"

Melanie sighed and blew her nose.

"No, I suppose not. But I've got to go into Exeter tomorrow afternoon to give them my formal statement, and until then, I don't know what to think."

"But what on earth could they think would be your motive? You're one of the stars of the upcoming production – although whether we go ahead with that now is anyone's guess. So why would you want to kill the musical director? She wasn't that much of a hard taskmistress, was she?"

"No, of course she wasn't. I quite enjoyed working with her. But what if the police hear the rumours about Edward? What if they're true? Won't they think that gives me a motive?"

"What rumours? For goodness sake, Melanie, what are you talking about?" She stopped and her eyes widened. "Isabella and Edward – you don't think…" Annie started laughing and then stopped hurriedly when she saw the look on Melanie's face. "Oh, darling, you're serious, aren't you? What on earth gave you that idea? Isabella and Edward, how ridiculous is that?"

"I heard two of the chorus chatting when I was tidying the music cupboard in the vestry on Saturday afternoon. They were talking about Isabella and her tenor."

"But Edward isn't the only tenor in the world. And he's not here most of the time."

"Yes, but he was acting so strangely last time he was here. Annie, I'm not sure he wants to get married at all. He can be really sweet, like when he was helping me rehearse my part last weekend. Then the next moment, when I suggested we look at the guest list for the reception, he went all cool on me and walked away. I thought he was regretting getting involved with a simple country lass, after all his sophisticated friends in London and around the world. And then I heard the gossip about him and Isabella. So now I don't know what to think."

"And what does Edward say about all this?"

"I haven't told him yet."

"What? Why not? He'd be down here like a shot to support you."

"Well, he's got a big concert later this week and I don't want to disturb him. Besides…" She stopped and bit her lip, her eyes filling with tears once again.

"Besides what, Melanie?"

"Oh, Annie, I don't know. What if the rumours are true?" She burst into tears again.

"What on earth's going on down there?" came a voice

from the top of the stairs. Suzy was standing on the landing. When she saw what was happening, she quickly ran down and wrapped her arms around Melanie. "Hey, Mel, come on, don't cry." She looked across at Annie. "What's the matter, Mama A?"

"Melanie's upset about Isabella, Suzy." She stood and brushed down the back of her jeans with her hand. "Can you take her upstairs and make her a coffee?" She glanced at her watch. "Look, I have to fly or Charlie will be wondering where I am. Melanie, there has to be a simple explanation for all this. Don't worry, we'll sort it all out." She paused and gave her daughter and her friend a joint hug. "But one thing I do know. We'll watch you walk down the aisle with your handsome tenor in the autumn. Because if we don't, I know a certain flower girl not a million miles from here who will never forgive us."

CHAPTER 24

Esther Steele's phone rang as she was putting the finishing touches to her latest commission, an arrangement of Alsatian pups frisking in the garden for a dog lover in Chudleigh. She dropped her brush in the jar of water and picked up her mobile.

"Yes, hello, Steele Farm."

"Esther, hi, it's Annie. How're you doing today?"

"I'm doing just fine, thanks. The sun's shining, the roses are budding and I'm going for a stroll around the village with my dad when he gets in from whatever he's doing in the bottom field this afternoon. How are you guys? How was your weekend away?"

"We're all well, thanks. And it was great. We took some smashing pictures in London. I'll show you next time I see you. But I was just ringing with this week's egg order. Can we have the usual?"

"Three dozen? Yes of course. And I've got some duck eggs as well, if you can use them."

"Oh yes please. They make wonderful omelettes."

"How's the preparation for *The Hero's Return* going? Is there any word yet on how Henry's going to manage without Isabella? Is it even going ahead?"

"No idea, I'm afraid. I think he's still recovering from

the shock. Plus he doesn't want to decide anything too quickly, out of respect for Isabella. There's a meeting tomorrow night and we'll know more then."

"It must have been a terrible shock for everyone."

"Especially poor Melanie."

"True." Esther shivered. "I can't imagine how I'd react in those circumstances. How's she doing?"

"Not well, to be honest. She's seeing the police this afternoon. She's really worried they might have her down as the principal suspect. Apparently it's something about killers returning to the scene of a murder?"

"What? That's a stupid idea. Poor Melanie."

"Yes, I know. And I'm sure she's got nothing to worry about. But to be honest, I'm thinking of getting the gang together again. Putting Charlie and Rohan on the case. See if we can shed some light on everything. Melanie's got some idea fixed in her head of a connection between Isabella and Edward, which she fears will be seen as a motive."

Esther bit her lip, wondering if she dared say what she was thinking.

"Esther, are you still there?" asked the voice at the other end of the line.

"Yes, sorry, Annie, I'm still here. I was just thinking. How would you like to get the others together here at the farm? It would be away from the village and give you a bit of peace and quiet to have your meeting."

"Oh, we couldn't bother you like that."

"Annie, I assure you, it would be no bother." She paused, knowing she was about to play her winning card. "And I'll even bake some of my little apple pies and ginger snaps to keep you all going while you're discussing your investigations."

"Well, if you're sure. That would be a great idea. Thank you. And I know how much the other two love your baking."

"And you don't?"

There was a chuckle from the other woman.

"Okay, you got me. I just love your apple pies." There was a pause. "Look, let me talk to the others and get back to you with some dates and times. And I'll see you tomorrow when I come to collect the eggs."

"Right you are. Bye, Annie."

As Esther picked up her paintbrush once again, she was humming to herself. This could be fun. She knew it was serious, and she was really sorry for young Melanie. After all, she knew how she felt when her father was in a similar situation the previous year. But part of her was really excited at the prospect of getting the three amateur sleuths back together in her kitchen.

The previous year she'd spent some fascinating afternoons sitting around the kitchen table with Annie, Charlie and Rohan. It was the first time she'd felt a member of a group for a very long time. And she'd loved being part of an investigation. She didn't think she was ready to accompany Rohan when he went on his enquiries. Although she hadn't had an anxiety attack for months and she was gradually getting used to going out and about with her father. But she did know she was good at paperwork and anything to do with computers. She'd realised during the previous investigation there was so much more they could have done if they'd set up a database and cross-referenced the information they'd gathered. Who knows, they might have come to a conclusion much faster.

The more she thought about it, the more Esther warmed to her idea. She'd start slowly, offering her kitchen for their meetings. And since Melanie was as much her friend as theirs, they weren't going to exclude her from their deliberations. Especially not in a kitchen rich with the aroma of freshly baked pastries and biscuits. Then all she would have to do was feed the information they gathered into her database and come up with a couple of connections they might otherwise have missed. And then she'd suggest they used her whenever they were investigating crimes. She doubted this would be the last time.

Esther stopped painting and told herself to slow down. It was all going so well in her head. But she knew it might not be so easy in reality. However, that didn't mean she wasn't going to try. If she had her way, before this murder investigation was over, Annie's gang of three would become a gang of four. And that would certainly qualify as the most interesting thing she'd done in a long time.

CHAPTER 25

Detective Constable Joanne Wellman's father always told her she'd make a great poker player. And as Derek Smith's voice droned on, she hoped she was managing to mask her thoughts effectively. It certainly wouldn't help her career chances if her superior officer knew she thought him boring and condescending. In fact, she quite liked Derek; he'd been happy to show her the ropes when she'd first joined the Major Crime Investigation Team, but ever since DCI Harolds had left for a new posting in the Midlands, there had been talk of promotions on the horizon. And DS Smith had his eye on the DI's spot.

"Okay, Jo, so we want you to take the lead on this interview – Melanie Unwin would probably be more relaxed talking to another woman. Use the witness room, it's more comfortable, and just take her through everything she can remember about Monday morning."

"Yes, Sarge."

"And don't forget she's a witness, not a suspect. At least for the time being."

"Yes, Sarge."

It was as though she'd never done this before, Joanne thought, but pasted a smile on her face as he continued.

"And don't mention the bloody candlestick unless she

does. We've not made that detail public so far."

At that moment, the front desk rang through to say Melanie Unwin had arrived. Joanne Wellman nodded to Derek Smith and headed off to collect their visitor.

"Ms Unwin, okay if I call you Melanie? I'm DC Wellman, Joanne. Thank you for coming in. We'll try not to take up too much of your time." She glanced around the empty foyer and pointed to a couple of easy chairs. "Shall we just have a chat before we go any further?" Melanie nodded. Once they were seated, Joanne continued. "I'm going to take your statement today. We'll do it in the witness suite, just through that door over there. If it's okay with you, we'll make a video recording of the interview. One of my colleagues will look after all that, so you won't even notice the camera is on. We can just chat everything through. Is that alright?"

"Yes, that's fine." Melanie's voice was little more than a whisper and she was twisting her hands tightly together as though trying to keep them from escaping. Joanne wondered if that was just a reaction to the stressful situation she found herself in or if the young woman had something to hide.

"Would you like a coffee before we start? Or maybe a few minutes to familiarise yourself with the room?"

Melanie pursed her lips and shook her head.

"No, I just want to get on with it, if that's okay. The sooner I can forget all about the past couple of days, the better." Her voice broke and she brushed a hand angrily across her eyes.

"Yes, of course it is. Come this way." Joanne led the way and left Melanie to settle herself while she went to check DS Smith was all set up in the adjoining video room. When she returned, she seated herself in the armchair across the coffee table from Melanie who was perched on the very edge of the matching sofa, looking around her.

"Pretty, isn't it?" asked Joanne, indicating the pale green walls and darker green tweed of the furniture. "We try to keep it looking informal." Melanie nodded, took a deep breath and smiled.

"Okay, DC Wellman, what do you want to know?"

"Well, why don't you start by telling me everything you can remember about Monday morning? Take your time. Just go through every little detail, even if it doesn't seem relevant."

By the time she'd finished telling the story, Melanie was shaking and looked close to tears once more.

"Do we know how she died – how she was killed, I mean?"

"Why do you think she was killed, Melanie?"

"Because the policeman said the death was suspicious, so I just assumed…"

Joanne Wellman nodded.

"Well, yes, we are considering it as a suspicious death, but we're still looking into all the circumstances." She paused. "You knew Isabella Street quite well, didn't you, Melanie?"

"Yes. I'm in the church choir that she led. And I'm singing in *The Hero's Return*. At least, I was. I'm not sure what's going to happen now."

"And was she an easy woman to get on with? Did she have anyone who would wish her harm?"

"She could be a bit of a tartar if we didn't get the music right, but generally, I think everyone got on with her." Melanie looked at Joanne with her head on one side. "You don't think it was someone who knew her, do you? Someone from the village?"

"We're keeping an open mind at the moment, Melanie." Joanne let that sink in for a moment before continuing. "Well, I think that's all for now. So unless there's anything else you would like to tell me…?" Melanie shook her head and picked up her bag. As she stood up, Joanne threw in one final question. "Sorry, just one thing I should have asked you. What made you go to the church that early on Monday morning?"

"What?" Melanie looked flustered and sat down again, dropping her bag back on the floor.

"Well, it was only just after seven. A bit early to expect to see anyone, wasn't it?"

"I wanted to talk to Rosemary."

"Reverend Leafield?"

"That's right. I knew she always opened the building first thing, and I needed her advice on something. So I thought I'd meet up with her and help open up."

"But she wasn't there?"

"No. Not until she heard the sirens and came to see what was happening."

"Okay, Melanie. You've been very helpful. We'll be in touch if we need anything else."

Joanne Wellman watched the young woman push her way through the front doors and hurry off towards the bus stop.

"There's something you're not telling me, Melanie Unwin," she murmured to herself as she headed back towards the MCIT office. "Now, I wonder what that might be?"

CHAPTER 26

"Come in, guys, grab a seat, the kettle's just boiled." Esther held open the kitchen door as Annie McLeod walked in, followed by her partner Charlie Jones, and their good friend Rohan Banerjee. Charlie was limping slightly and lowered herself into one of the two rocking chairs by the fireplace with a grateful sigh. "Charlie, what's the matter? You look in pain."

"Oh, it's nothing really, Esther. An old war wound. It plays me up a bit when it's damp outside."

Annie let out a gentle snort and put her hand on her partner's shoulder.

"Old war wound, my foot!" She shook her head. "She's pulled a muscle giving Suzy a piggyback in the beer garden. I told her our daughter's far too big for that now. But it's the old ones who're the most stubborn, you know." She blew a kiss at Charlie to soften her words as she took a seat at the kitchen table.

"What do you mean, old?" growled Charlie indignantly. "I'm not sixty yet. And I can still give most of the youngsters in the village a run for their money." She paused, put her hands on the small of her back and stretched. "But I must admit, I'm feeling every year of my age today." She stood and joined Annie at the table. "I think I'll have a good soak in the bath when we get home."

Rohan and Esther had been standing by the door, watching this interplay with smiles on their faces. Now, the young private detective joined his friends at the table while Esther moved across to the Aga. Soon there was a delicious aroma of fresh coffee mingling with the already present smell of baking. She picked up the tray and joined them at the table.

"I must say this is a refreshingly different way to spend an afternoon," said Rohan, biting into one of Esther's famous apple pies.

"Have you been busy lately, Rohan?" asked their host, handing around the coffee.

"So-so." The young man grimaced. "It's amazing how many dogs and husbands go astray while on holiday at the seaside. But this is a different level of case, isn't it?"

"Yes," said Annie. "I explained briefly what this was about when I set up the meeting but let me give you all the details as I have them." She went on to relate her conversation with Melanie and why the young woman was so upset and worried. "And after her interview in Exeter yesterday, I don't think she's any more reassured. She's convinced the police are going to treat her as a suspect. Plus of course, there's this ridiculous idea she's got into her head about Isabella and Edward."

"So where are you going to start?" asked Esther, picking up a Sharpie from the table and standing next to her easel, which she'd set up to the side with a large sheet of paper tacked to it. "You talk and I'll write."

They all looked at Rohan. After all, he was the professional in the room. He smiled and stood up, walking backwards and forwards with his hands behind his back, much to Esther's amusement.

"Well, Annie, you're best placed to talk to all the singers. Find out how much they know about what Isabella's been up to in the past few weeks." Esther wrote 'Annie – Choir' at the top of the sheet as Rohan went on. "I'm afraid you're going to have to tackle the two gossips in particular. You'd better not tell them Melanie overheard them that day. We don't want to give people the idea she's in the habit of hiding – especially not in the church."

"Right, will do." Annie threw a mock salute.

"Charlie, you see Henry Whitehead most nights in the pub, don't you?"

"Eight-thirty every evening, regular as clockwork, rain or shine. He always calls in for a pint of best ale when he's taken Bertie for his walk."

"Well you work on him then. Find out if there's anything in this blessed opera thing of theirs that could've led to murder."

"*The Hero's Return?* Can't see how, but yes, of course I will."

"And I'll take a look into the other aspects of Isabella's life. That landlady of hers should certainly be worth a look."

As they talked, Esther kept jotting things down on her makeshift flip chart. When they'd finished their initial plans, she coughed shyly and then picked up her laptop and placed it on the table.

"If you've finished your planning for now, can I show you guys something?" She opened the laptop, hit a few keys, and then beckoned them to join her at the end of the table. "I put this together after you finished working on the events of last year." She didn't need to elaborate more than that. They would all know she was referring to the investigation they'd carried out leading to the solving not only of two contemporary murders, but also clearing up the disappearance of her own mother when Esther was just a child.

Charlie, who had a background in computing among other things, looked at the screen and whistled. Annie and Rohan looked perplexed, and Charlie grinned.

"Esther, I know exactly what this is, but perhaps you could explain for the benefit of these two computer illiterates here?"

"It's a database. A way of storing facts and cross-referencing data."

Annie and Rohan looked at each other and shrugged. Esther went on.

"I plugged in all the data you guys collected during your investigations. It quickly highlighted areas where there was information missing. And it also allowed me to make connections we might've missed first time around."

Charlie took up the story.

"For example, it took us quite a while to find out who Amelia really was and identify her links to the other people in the case. We might have got to the end point more quickly if we'd been asking questions more systematically and got the answers faster. Who knows, we might even have stopped the second murder from taking place."

Esther watched as the light finally dawned on the faces of the other two.

"So, what you're saying," said Rohan, "is that we could use this now, right from the start, and hopefully get to the answers we need more quickly? Esther, that's brilliant."

"What a wonderful idea. Esther, you are clever," said Annie.

"So I was wondering," said Esther, feeling very shy all of a sudden, "if I could help you with your investigations." She paused and bit her lip. "I hope it doesn't sound terrible to say this, but despite the circumstances, I enjoyed working with you guys last year, going through all the facts you collected. I just wanted to do it all again."

Annie reached down and gave their friend and host a hug. Then she looked at Charlie and Rohan.

"What do you think, guys? I vote yes. We need someone to organise us and keep us in order." There were enthusiastic nods from the other two.

"On one condition," said Rohan. "We use the farm as our HQ. And Esther combines the role of data analyst with baker!"

There were laughs and hugs all around as the deal was

cemented.

CHAPTER 27

Realising it was time for Suzy to arrive home from school, Charlie and Annie headed back to The Falls. Rohan offered them a lift, but they were happy to walk down the lane, despite Charlie's aches and pains.

"I think the walk'll do me good," she said, as she hugged her friends and followed Annie across the farmyard.

Rohan folded up the easel and returned it to Esther's studio, then helped her clear the table, washing and drying the mugs before putting them back on the hooks on the dresser.

"Would you like another coffee?" asked Esther. "And maybe another apple pie?"

"No, thanks. You must be busy, getting ready for Tommy's supper."

"Not for ages yet. In fact I've nothing at all to do for the next hour. So do stay and keep me company." Esther wasn't at all surprised to hear the young man accept. She had a suspicion he was in no hurry to return to his empty bedsit in Teignmouth. She quickly made a fresh pot of coffee and the two sat in the rocking chairs by the fireplace.

"So, Rohan, how's the business really going?"

"Oh, you know. As I said, lots of lost husbands and dogs. I'm doing okay." Esther cocked an eyebrow at him but said nothing. Finally, he sighed and shook his head. "I'm not fooling you, am I, Esther? The situation is pretty dire. I only had one case last month. I can barely pay the rent. And running my car is getting very difficult. In fact, if it wasn't for the occasional shifts I get at Cosy Café and The Falls, I'd be completely broke. And even that's not ideal, as there's so much travelling involved. My car's on its last legs. I don't see it getting through the next MOT. So that's another concern." He pulled a face and shook his head again. "To be quite honest, I'm thinking I'll have to give it all up and take a proper job. Maybe a security guard in one of the clubs in Exeter or Torquay. Something like that."

"But you'd hate that, surely. Working for someone else after being your own boss."

"True, I'd find it very difficult. But you know what they say about beggars…"

Esther stared at her guest and wondered if she dared say what was in her mind. She decided it was worth a try.

"You could always come and live here."

"What, here at the farm?"

"Yes. Later this year, we'll be doing up some of the outbuildings, turning them into accommodation. We'll be looking for tenants. There'd be space for you to live and to work. And the rent would be much less than you're paying now."

"But that's going to be months away. I don't think I can wait that long."

"So move in here in the meantime. This place is massive. Dad and I rattle around here on our own. There's plenty of space."

"But how would your father take to that idea?"

"He'd love it. He may seem quiet and moody to other people, but I know him better than anyone else – anyone living anyway. And since we found out what happened to my mother, he's started to become much more sociable once again. I'm sure he'd love some company in the evenings." She paused and wondered if she was pushing him too hard. "Not that you'd be tied to the place or anything. You'd be free to come and go as you please."

Rohan smiled at her and nodded his head slowly.

"Well, I must say the idea has great appeal. I'd be closer to you guys for our investigation. And I'd be within walking distance of Cosy Corner and The Falls."

"And we always have a couple of spare vehicles here at the farm. You could use one of those until things looked up and you were able to buy a new one."

"And I guess I could help on the farm on days when I wasn't busy. Does your dad ever need extra hands?"

"You could even do some of the work on the conversion site if you like. How are you with a paintbrush?"

"Not bad. Not bad at all. In fact, I spent a couple of summers on a building site as a teenager before I joined the force. I used to be quite good with the old plaster and trowel."

The two looked at each other and laughed. Esther felt a warm glow at the thought of having someone closer to her own age to talk to daily. She was gradually starting to go out and about, following the subsidence of her anxiety attacks, but she still spent far more time than she wanted to alone in the farm. Suddenly it looked as if that might be changing.

But then Rohan's face changed.

"Esther, this all sounds absolutely wonderful. And I'll be delighted if it comes off. But there's one thing you must do first, and that's to talk to your father. You say he's getting more sociable and will enjoy the company. But would your father really want a stranger living in his house?"

Esther grinned and nodded her head.

"I'm absolutely sure he'll be happy with the idea. He keeps telling me I should get more friends, have people around here more of the time. I don't think there'll be a problem. Let me talk to him tonight when he gets in." She looked at the calendar. "How much notice do you have to give on your place in Teignmouth? A month?"

"Two weeks, I think."

"Right, well, I'll talk to my dad tonight and get back to you in the morning. You should be able to move in here before the end of the month."

CHAPTER 28

"To Isabella. May she rest in peace." Amanda Bosworth raised her glass and looked around the bar of The Falls at the assembled crowd. Everyone was there, apart from Henry Whitehead. He'd been the one to arrange this informal wake and she assumed he'd be there very soon. Once he'd finished taking his dog for a walk probably.

"To Isabella."

"To Bella."

"Rest in peace, Bella."

The murmurs came from around the room.

"And may the bastard who killed her rot in hell!" It was said quietly, and Amanda thought it came from one of the tenors. It wasn't the language she'd normally use. But she knew it was a sentiment echoed by everyone there. So she decided to let it pass. Taking a sip of her drink before placing her glass on the table, she walked to the centre of the room, glancing at the huge clock behind the bar as she did so. It was eight-twenty in the evening.

"Right, guys. Henry's due to be here and I assume he'll arrive very soon, but in the meantime, let's get started on the main point of discussion. After the tragic events of last weekend, what happens next?"

"Well, we carry on, don't we?" asked one of the

sopranos.

"You're not suggesting we give up, are you?" This from a bass leaning against the bar in the corner.

"It's what Isabella would have wanted," another of the sopranos chipped in. "And it would be a tribute to her, as well as a celebration of Henry's relative," she looked around the bar and raised her hands as everyone joined in, "Great-great-great-uncle Aubrey." There was a ripple of laughter, with which Amanda joined in. She stopped abruptly however, as the door opened and Henry Whitehead stumbled in, followed by Bertie, his little Jack Russell terrier. Henry's coat was hanging open and his tie was awry. This wasn't the Henry Whitehead they were used to seeing.

"Henry, come on over here. Charlie, a glass of the usual for Henry, please." Amanda nudged the singer next to her who rapidly stood and offered his chair to the new arrival.

"Thank you, Amanda. Sorry I'm late. I was walking Bertie as usual, and a question came into my mind about the staging. I was halfway to Isabella's cottage to chat it through with her before I remembered…" He broke off and bit his lip, blinking rapidly. Thinking how old and frail he looked, Amanda put her arm around his shoulders and gave him a quick squeeze.

"I know, Henry, I know. We all miss her." Then clearing her throat, she stepped back into the circle and raised her voice. "Okay, guys. To make sure I understand, and to bring Henry up to date, you're all adamant you want to continue with the production of *The Hero's Return* as originally scheduled?"

There was a groundswell of sound as each person nodded, clapped their hands, tapped the table in front of them, or otherwise indicated their agreement. Henry stood up and joined Amanda in the centre of the room.

"I can't tell you how grateful I am to hear you say that." His voice broke and he cleared his throat before continuing. "I heard someone saying it's what dear Isabella would have wanted. And I quite agree. So, you have my full support moving forward, and the financing for the project will remain in place." He turned and looked at Gavin Porter who was sitting on a stool at the end of the bar. "You're very quiet, Gavin. Can we rely on your ongoing involvement?"

Amanda held her breath and watched as the young tenor shrugged his shoulders, then slowly started shaking his head.

"Actually, Henry, I don't think you can." There was a gasp from someone at the edge of the crowd, and Gavin flushed slightly as he continued. "Look, we all know it wasn't working out. I told Isabella I wasn't right for the role. And," he said, looking pointedly at Amanda, "I'm pretty sure I wasn't the only one who tried to persuade her to replace me. So I'm going to make it easy for all of you and step down now. I'm going to have to get out of the cottage, anyway, I suspect. Penelope Conway is sure to want it back." He picked up his pint glass and drained it in one long gulp then jumped down from his stool and pulled on his jacket. "So I think I'm going to head back to the family farm in Wales, spend some time with my folks, and take a long hard look at my life." And with a wave of his hand, he headed through the door and out into the night.

Amanda stared at Henry in silence. She was pretty sure his main feeling, like hers, would be one of relief. But she wasn't going to put that into words. Not out here in public anyway.

"So how're we going to organise this?" The question came from Annie who'd been listening to everything going on from the public side of the bar for once. "You're not here all the time, Amanda. And, Henry, you're not a musician." Looking around the bar and indicating her fellow members of the choir, she went on, "We're all amateurs; but we want to make sure we do you and Isabella proud. We need someone to lead us in our rehearsals."

"I wonder if I might help with that?"

There was silence as a stranger stepped forward from the corner of the bar. Amanda had noticed him when she first arrived but had never seen him before. Henry looked at the newcomer in surprise.

"And you are?"

"The name's Henning, Michael Henning." He held out his hand to Henry and then to Amanda. "I'm an old friend of Isabella Street, back from our university days. We lost touch many years ago and I'd only recently found out she was living in this part of the world. I'm devastated to have lost her once again – and in such a terrible way."

"Yes, it was awful, wasn't it," said Amanda. "We're all trying to come to terms with her death ourselves." She paused, bowing her head in silent tribute to their departed MD, before looking back up at the newcomer. "You said you could help with the choir," said Amanda. "Are you a singer, then? Or a musician?"

"Actually, I'm both. Although these days it's a passionate hobby rather than anything else. But I've worked with choirs all my adult life and I had the privilege of hearing this wonderful group of singers when I visited Isabella one day last week. They're right to want to carry on; and I can help them." He paused and made a small expression of humility. "If you and they will have me, that is."

"Well, I'm sure that would be wonderful," said Henry, rubbing his hands together. "Let's sit over there and I'll go through the rehearsal schedule with you."

As they walked away, Henry talking and Michael Henning nodding enthusiastically, Amanda couldn't help wondering if this unexpected turn of events was completely providential.

"Just one thing, Mr Henning," she called across the bar. "Isabella Street's music was very special and quite unique. How familiar are you with her style?"

"Oh, trust me, Ms Bosworth," came the immediate reply, "I'm very familiar with dear Isabella's composition style. Very familiar indeed."

CHAPTER 29

Tommy Steele pushed his chair back from the table and sighed contentedly.

"Another wonderful supper, Esther. Thank you, my love," he said. "You've certainly inherited your mum's talent in the kitchen." He stood up and stretched, then walked to the window. The sun was disappearing behind the distant hills. "How do you fancy a stroll before it goes completely dark? We can clear up the dishes when we get back."

"Sure. Why not." Esther pushed her phone into her pocket and picked up the leads. Tinker, her father's dog, pranced around her, falling over his own feet in his eagerness to be outside once again. Frisk, her much older pet, ambled across from his bed in the corner and stood patiently waiting his turn. "You don't really need this, do you, old boy," she said, gently ruffling his fur. "But Tinker will only whine if he's on the lead and you aren't."

As the pair strolled across the farmyard, heading for the open fields and the hill down towards the barns, Esther hooked her arm through her father's.

"There's something I want to talk to you about," she said. "And I want you to think carefully before you answer." Despite her earlier confidence when assuring Rohan, she suddenly wondered if maybe her suggestion might not go down as well as she'd anticipated.

Tommy stopped walking and turned to face his daughter.

"That sounds very serious. You're not ill again, are you?" Being ill had always been his way of describing her panic attacks. She laughed and patted his arm.

"No, Dad, it's nothing like that. I'm absolutely fine, and getting better every day. In fact, I even went into Chudleigh on my own today and did some shopping. Then I had lunch in Harveys. And I didn't panic once!"

Tommy put his hand on his chest and exhaled deeply.

"Phew, that's good to hear. I was a bit worried there, for a minute." He started walking again. "So what's this subject you want me to think seriously about, then?"

"I'm wondering if we can take in a lodger?"

"But we've talked about that. It's already been agreed. As soon as the lads can fit in time to do the conversion, we'll have those units available." He looked puzzled. "You hadn't forgotten, had you?"

"No, Dad, I hadn't forgotten. But that's going to take a while, isn't it? This needs to be a bit quicker than that. I've got a friend who's in a bit of a pickle, running out of money, with a business that's not too good and a car that's about to expire. It would be great if we could lend a hand. And we've got loads of room in the farmhouse. What do you think?"

"Of course we can. What's her name?"

"Er, it's not a her. It's a him. It's Rohan Banerjee. You remember that friend of Charlie and Annie?"

"That young detective who helped solve the mystery of your mother's death? Yes, of course I remember him. He was in the pub the other week when we went in for supper. Nice young chap, he is. I'm sorry to hear he's having a bad time of it."

"So you wouldn't mind if he stayed with us for a while? He'd need a bedroom, of course, and maybe somewhere to set up his laptop. Most of his work's online or out in the field. But he'd eat with us. I was thinking of charging him just for the cost of his meals for the moment. That'll help with his cash flow. And he reckons he's a dab hand with plastering and painting."

"Well, in that case, I should think we can find plenty of ways he can earn his keep." Her father paused to examine an early flower peeping out of the hedgerow. "In fact, if he's going to be working on the conversions with us, he can design his own unit. Make sure it suits his needs."

Esther was delighted at the enthusiastic way her father had taken to her suggestion. She hugged herself at the thought of having another person her own age around the place, at least some of the time. Things were certainly starting to look up for her.

"So when's he moving in, this young man of yours?" Her father's voice pulled her out of her reverie.

"What? Oh, around the end of the month, I think. He needs to give two weeks' notice on his current place. And I'll need time to air one of the spare rooms. I'm going to give him the one with the basin in the corner. It's not as good as a full en-suite, but it's a start." Then she stopped dead as the impact of her father's words hit her. She felt a flush rising on her cheeks and was glad it was too dark for her father to see her face. "Oh no, Dad. It's nothing like that. He's not 'my young man'. He's just a friend who's in trouble; a friend who helped us out last year and who hopefully will find life a little easier if we can give him a hand in return." She paused, searching for words to stop her father's thoughts before they progressed further down that route. "And it's only going to be temporary, anyway. As soon as the units are converted, he'll be able to move into one of those and we'll have our place back to ourselves." She shook her head. "I'm not interested in that sort of thing."

"It's alright, Esther, I was only joking." Her father patted her arm. "Although, there really is nothing wrong with the idea of you starting to think about 'that sort of thing', as you put it. It wasn't feasible before now. But I'm not daft enough to think you'll want to spend the rest of your life looking after an old man like me." He pulled on the lead to retrieve Tinker from the undergrowth before turning back for the farmhouse. "Right, I think it's time we got back and put the kettle on. It'll be time for the news pretty soon."

As she followed him back up the lane towards the farmhouse, Esther felt the breeze cooling her cheeks. And she wondered if her father would be the only one to misread the situation. She had a sudden thought. What if Rohan had thought her suggestion too forward? What if he'd already changed his mind? She'd better make sure when she phoned him in the morning he didn't think she had an ulterior motive for suggesting this new living arrangement.

CHAPTER 30

"Rohan, can you see if Celia and Roger are ready to order?" Charlie turned as she waited for the latest of several dozen pint glasses to fill with local ale, and called out to her temporary barman for the evening. Annie had offered to help out, but Charlie knew she'd want to concentrate on the discussion about the future of the choir, so she'd drafted in their friend instead. This way, they also had three pairs of eyes on the group that realistically had a good chance of including Isabella's killer.

"Yes, sure."

Charlie watched as the young man trotted down the corridor and into the restaurant area, which was considerably quieter than the crowded bar. She noted he seemed a lot brighter than when they'd all gathered that afternoon in Esther's kitchen. That was good. She didn't like to see their friend looking so miserable. She knew times were difficult for him and wished there was more they could do to help. He was soon back, heading for the kitchen, pad in hand.

"You'll never guess…" he said with a grin in passing.

"Roger's having the steak, medium rare with triple cooked chips and no tomatoes."

"Spot on. Celia's going to give tonight's special a try, but you know Roger. He knows what he likes and sees no reason to change." Rohan's voice dropped an octave and took on a Devon burr as he imitated the regular saying of the proprietor of Cosy Corner. But there was no malice in his voice and Charlie knew a deep bond of friendship had developed between Rohan Banerjee and the Richardsons. Celia in particular looked on Rohan as the son she'd never had.

When the meals were ready, Charlie left the bar for a moment to help Rohan carry everything in.

"I must say you're looking a lot brighter tonight, me lover," said Celia. "Proper glum you were last time we saw you."

"Yes, I was thinking the same," said Charlie. "Have you got yourself a new client?"

"Not a new client, no, unless you count the work we're doing for Melanie. But I've got some good news." Rohan smiled at the three of them and took a deep breath. "Esther and Tommy are planning on converting some of their old buildings into accommodation and I'm going to have one of them, with space to run the agency from home. It'll be cheaper than the place I've got now, and I'll be able to walk to the centre of the village when I'm working for you guys. My car's on its last legs, and I've been really worried about getting stranded down in Teignmouth. Esther says I can probably borrow one of the farm vehicles if I need to go out on a job. Just until I can get myself a new set of wheels."

"Rohan, that's great news." Celia dropped her napkin on the table and jumped to her feet. "Come and give me a hug." She gathered him into her arms, as Roger and Charlie exchanged an amused glance. Being enveloped by Celia was no small matter.

"But it's going to take a while for the conversion to happen. So I guess you're stuck where you are for a few months yet?" Roger was always the practical one. Rohan cleared his throat and put a finger to his lips.

"Well, it's not settled yet, so don't say anything, but I'm

hoping to be moving in the next couple of weeks. Esther suggested I lodge with them at the farm until the conversion's done. Apparently they've got loads of space. And I'm going to be able to help with the conversion work too."

"Are you sure Tommy's okay with that?" Celia looked concerned. "He's not the most sociable of folks, you know."

"Completely sure. Or, at least, Esther is. Seems he's regaining some of his earlier sociability now he finally knows what happened to June all those years ago. She's going to talk to him tonight."

"Well, that's really good news," Celia said once more. "I'm delighted for you."

"Looks like you've fallen on your feet there, Rohan, my lad." Roger winked at him. "And who knows, maybe your young woman and her father will turn you into a farmer too. Getting your feet under that table could be quite lucrative all round."

"Oh, no, Roger, it's nothing like that." Charlie watched with interest as Rohan flushed hotly. "Esther and I are just friends. I met her through Charlie and Annie; and she's grateful for the help I gave her last year after her mother's body was discovered." He shook his head. "No, she's just helping me out. That's all."

"Well, if you say so, lad. That may be how you see it. But what about her? Are you sure that's how she reads the situation too?"

"Roger, you are awful," said his wife, playfully swatting at his arm. "Stop teasing him." She turned to Rohan. "Ignore him. He's just being funny – or at least, he thinks he is."

At that point, someone rang the bell hanging in the bar. Charlie glanced at her watch. It was nowhere near closing time.

"Sounds like the crowd's getting restless in there. I'd better get back. Rohan, when you've finished in here, perhaps you can come and help me? It looks like it's going to be another long, busy night."

As she left the restaurant and returned to the bar, Charlie glanced over her shoulder. Celia and Roger were tucking into their food and chatting quietly. Rohan, on the other hand, was standing with a tray in his hand, staring out of the window with a slight frown on his face. Charlie grinned and looked forward to bringing Annie up to date on their friend's news when she got her to herself later on. But for now, there were glasses to fill and crisps to hand across the bar. She hoped Rohan wouldn't spend too long in contemplation. She really needed that extra pair of hands tonight.

CHAPTER 31

The last of the choir members drifted away around eleven-fifteen. Annie was helping Charlie and Rohan with the clearing up. Amanda and Henry sat nursing their last drinks in front of the fire.

"I do miss her, you know," said Henry, putting down his glass and pulling a large chequered handkerchief out of his pocket. He blew his nose and looked at Amanda through red-rimmed eyes that were watering. "We've been friends ever since she came to the village."

Amanda nodded and placed her hand on the old man's arm.

"I know, Henry. I've not known her as long as you, of course. And she could be stubborn if she got an idea into her head…"

"Like Gavin?"

"Like Gavin, precisely. But her heart was in the right place. And she certainly wrote some beautiful music."

"Yes, her music." Henry gave a deep sigh. "It was nice of the choir to say they want to continue with *The Hero's Return*. But, I'm not sure. Is it going to work? Are we going to get everything ready in time for the anniversary? Maybe we should postpone? We've only got a couple of weeks left."

111

"Well, before this evening, I might have agreed with you, Henry. But after hearing the enthusiasm among the singers, I think we might just have a chance."

"But without Gavin?"

"Pooh, we can replace Gavin pretty easily. You've arranged for the funding to continue, so it shouldn't be too difficult."

"I'd thought of asking Edward if he could recommend anyone we could approach. Or even if he would consider singing the role himself."

"Edward Jennings? Oh no, I wouldn't have thought we're in that league at all, Henry. And surely Edward's too old for the part?"

Henry looked at her in silence for a moment and raised an eyebrow. Amanda felt herself going pink. Then she laughed and shrugged her shoulders.

"Okay, fair point. And if you can have a fifty-year-old soprano singing Madame Butterfly in Covent Garden, I don't see why anyone would object to a rather mature couple singing Aubrey and Cissie. And if Edward would consider it, he'd be a wonderful draw." She paused. "Would you like me to have a word with him?"

"No, I thought we'd ask Annie to do that. After all, she and Charlie are very close to Melanie."

"Good idea. We'll talk to them when they've finished clearing up."

Henry cleared his throat.

"But it's not just the lead singer we need to replace, is it? There's the small matter of the musical director. What do you think of this Henning chap?"

Amanda took a sip of her drink. She didn't want to lose this part. So it was in her own interests for Michael Henning to take on the role of musical director. But she didn't want Henry to think she was pushing him into anything. Much better if he came to the decision all on his own.

"Well," she said, putting her glass back down on the table, "he certainly seems confident he can do it."

"And he obviously knows Isabella's music well, from the way he was talking about their days together in Newcastle."

"But, it's your baby, Henry. What do you think about taking him on? What do you think Isabella would want you to do?"

"Oh, without a doubt, she'd want the production to go ahead. She was as passionate about it as I am."

"And Michael Henning?"

"I really don't know. There's no reason to think she wouldn't want him involved. After all, they were very close at one time, apparently." He stared into the fire for a long moment. Amanda was wondering if he'd dozed off. Then he sat up with a start. "Well, I guess we'll never know. But I think we'll give him the benefit of the doubt, hmm?" He nodded to himself a couple of times and pulled a thin piece of card from his waistcoat pocket. "Yes, I'll ring him first thing tomorrow and confirm that we are happy to accept his offer."

CHAPTER 32

"Rohan Banerjee speaking. Your problems are my business. How may I help you?"

Esther grinned at the sound of the voice at the other end of the line. If projects were given out on the basis of enthusiasm, then Rohan's new investigation agency should be booming.

"Hi, Rohan, it's Esther. Not too early to call you, is it?" Glancing at the clock as she waited for the call to go through, she'd remembered belatedly that not everyone rose as early as farming families, and although breakfast was finished in her household it was still before eight o'clock.

"No, you're fine, Esther. I've been up for ages. I've just come back from my run. What can I do for you?"

"I wanted to let you know straight away. My dad's really happy at the idea of you taking one of the units once they're ready. And when I told him you were willing to help with the building work, he was even more delighted. In fact, he's suggested you design your unit yourself. That way, it will be just how you like it." She paused. "And, he's agreed you can stay with us in the meantime."

"Hey, that's great news. Do thank him from me, won't you?"

"Well, you can thank him yourself. I wondered if you'd

114

like to come over for supper one day next week so we can finalise all the details?"

"Sounds good. I'm doing a couple of shifts in the café. How about Tuesday? I could be there around six-thirty?"

"Perfect. We don't eat until eight-ish, so that'll give me time to show you around."

There was a long pause and Esther wondered if the connection had been lost. She bit her tongue and then decided she had to say what was on her mind. But as she spoke, so did Rohan.

"My dad…"

"Roger…"

They both stopped, then started again.

"After you…"

"No, you first."

There was another pause then Esther gave a nervous laugh.

"This is embarrassing, but I'm just going to go on and say it so there'll be no misunderstanding." She swallowed. "My dad seems to think there's something going on between us. I've told him we're just friends, but I wanted to warn you in case he says anything when you meet him."

Rohan laughed.

"Funny you should say that. I was just about to mention that Roger Richardson has got the same idea in his head. Celia's told him to behave himself and stop being silly, but if he says anything when you go into the café, just ignore him. I haven't given him any reason to believe anything different, I promise you."

"I guess that's the problem with living in a small village," said Esther with a sigh. "Everyone knows your business. Or at least they think they do."

"And if they don't, they'll make it up anyway," agreed Rohan.

"You're sure you want to put yourself through this?"

"What, move into a comfortable room with space to work and the opportunity to enjoy home cooking while helping to design and build my own home? Sounds perfect to me." He paused then went on, "Unless you're having second thoughts of course. You've enough to do looking after your dad and the others, plus your work. If you think taking on a lodger is going to be too much for you, do say, won't you?"

Esther giggled happily.

"I'm not having second thoughts at all. As you say, I'm cooking for a crowd most days, so another one won't make any difference. And I'm looking forward to the extra company, to be honest."

"Right, that's settled then. I'll see you around six-thirty pm on Tuesday. And I'll bring some of that red wine you said your dad likes. And in the meantime, I'll get my notice handed in down here and start thinking about packing up my stuff. See you on Tuesday, Esther. And thank you again. You've saved my life."

He disconnected the call. Esther stood staring at the handset for a few minutes before dropping it on the table. She hugged herself and pirouetted around the room. Frisk stared up at her from his basket by the fireplace and gave a little whine, as though asking if everything was okay. She dropped to her knees and put her hands either side of his face. Well on in years now, the old dog was more grey and white than anything else, but his eyes were as bright as ever. Esther stroked his silky head and dropped a kiss on his nose. "We're getting a new friend, Frisk. It might not be quite as quiet around here in future, but it's certainly going to be more interesting." She got to her feet and walked to the sink, picking up the kettle as she passed the Aga. As she turned on the tap, she hummed a little tune to herself. "Yes, Frisk, I think I can definitely say things are going to be more interesting around here from now on."

CHAPTER 33

Two days after the wake, Michael Henning stood at the front of the church and faced the choir for the first time. From the way he was clasping and unclasping his hands, Annie surmised he was feeling just a tad nervous. She could understand why. It must be daunting to take over an established group like this, so close to the performance date; particularly given the circumstances leading up to the vacancy. She couldn't help feeling sorry for him and hoped the more disruptive elements of the choir wouldn't give him a hard time.

But she quickly found she was worrying unnecessarily.

"No, no, no!" Michael Henning waved his arms impatiently and the singing came to a ragged halt. "Come on, altos, it's quite simple. You should be able to do this in your sleep." He exhaled sharply. "Right, everyone else take a break; have a drink while we go through the alto part one more time."

They'd been working on this one piece for more than half an hour and it seemed to be getting worse not better. Annie was certainly struggling to make the difficult key change at the start of the second verse. The sopranos, perfectly happy with their straightforward main theme, smiled in sympathy as they went to get their drinks, although one or two looked smug rather than sympathetic.

"Hmm. Not sure I'm liking this style of rehearsal," murmured Melanie in Annie's ear.

"No. Isabella was firm with us. But she never shouted. And she was very patient."

"We're going to have to practise this one on our own time, aren't we, Annie?"

"I think you're right. I wonder if we could get our new MD to provide us with a soundtrack to work to?"

Melanie stifled a giggle.

"Well, you can ask him, if you like. I'm not going to risk upsetting him. I've still got my solo to sing for him."

"Oh, you'll be fine. Edward's been working with you on it, hasn't he?"

"Yes. I guess so."

Annie realised Melanie didn't sound so sure about Edward's help. But at that moment, Michael rapped his baton on the music stand.

"Right, ladies. From bar 29. And let's try to get it right this time, shall we?"

By the end of two hours, everyone was feeling wrung out. Their new musical director closed his score and smiled at the assembled singers.

"Okay, folks, that'll do for this evening." He paused and then nodded his head. "I know some of you probably think I was too hard on you," looking at the altos in particular, "but I wanted to see how far I could push you all. I have to say I'm very impressed. Isabella has done a wonderful job so far, and I firmly believe we can pull off a performance she would have been proud of."

There were looks of surprise and gratification across the faces of the choir. Annie looked at Melanie and raised her eyebrows. She wasn't a fan of the harsh school of coaching. Although she had to admit they'd been sounding pretty good by the end of the rehearsal. Michael Henning continued.

"Look, I know this is a difficult situation for all of us.

Made even worse by Isabella's tragic death. So I've a suggestion to make. How do you all fancy a day out next Sunday? The forecast's good, so I was thinking we could maybe go for a walk up on Dartmoor. Take a picnic lunch and then finish back in The Falls for a couple of drinks and some supper. My treat. What do you think?"

Some of the singers had prior engagements and declined the offer, but most of the choir seemed to think it was a great idea. As the group broke up, there were lots of excited conversations about lift sharing and who was going to bring what for the picnic.

"You head off, Michael, you've got further to go home than the rest of us." Annie could see the new musical director was unsure of what to do about closing the church for the evening. "Melanie and I will sort it."

"Are you sure? I'm happy to wait until you've finished. Especially since…"

"No, you're fine." Melanie bit her lip. "I was really nervous about coming back in here to start with. But I'm not letting a random act of violence scare me into changing how I behave. And this church is such a big part of my life. I can't possibly NOT spend time in here." She paused and grinned. "Besides, I've got Annie here with me." Annie saw Michael glance across at her sceptically and smiled as her friend continued. "She may look tiny and harmless, but Annie and Charlie have a history you wouldn't believe. I feel very safe with her in my corner."

"Sounds fascinating. Maybe you can tell me next Sunday?" He gathered his score together and tucked his music case under his arm. "Well, if you're really sure, I'll take you up on your offer. The roads should be clear at this time of night, but it'll still take a while to get back to Torquay. Thanks for all your hard work tonight, ladies. See you on Tuesday night for the next rehearsal." And with a mock salute, Michael Henning walked down the aisle and out of the church. Annie and Melanie watched him go.

"Well, what do you think of our new leader?" asked

Melanie.

"Not sure. He seems pleasant enough, but there were some definite moments tonight when we saw a different side to him." Annie folded the music stand and stowed it in the vestry. "Yes, I'd say the jury's still out on our Mr Michael Henning." She looked at her watch. "Right, let's get out of here. Charlie will be wondering where I've got to."

CHAPTER 34

Penny Conway couldn't wait to get away. She'd only popped into Cosy Corner for a slice of Celia's broccoli quiche and to stock up on a few things from the grocery counter. But it'd been a mistake. She should have used one of the shops in Chudleigh, where no-one knew her. Here in Coombesford, everyone knew her name and her business.

"I'm so sorry for your loss, lovey," Celia had said when she'd first arrived in the shop. For one horrible moment, Penny thought the other woman was going to try to hug her, but she'd fixed her with a glare and the moment passed. "Such a wonderful woman, was our Bella. And the way she looked after your mum. She was an absolute saint. You must be devastated."

Penny had bit her tongue hard at that. She suspected the villagers blamed her for not spending more time with her mum during her last years. But they had no idea how difficult she'd been. No idea at all. And as for the sainted Isabella Street, she'd had a cushy digs for years, followed by a very good deal on the cottage after Penny's mother died. She'd got more than a decent reward for a few months of caring.

Penny sat on the green in the surprisingly strong spring sunshine and watched the ducks on the pond as she munched on her lunch. Then she shook the crumbs from the front of her leather trousers, squared her shoulders and prepared to do battle over the cottage once more.

But in fact it was much easier than she'd expected it to be.

Gavin Porter opened the front door as soon as she walked through the squeaky gate. He must have been watching for her out of the window.

"I know what you're going to say," he began as she walked up the path towards him. "You need me out. Well, I'm nearly all packed up. I can be gone later today. I just want to clear up the kitchen, get rid of anything that won't keep – "

"No, laddie, you don't have to do that." Penny suddenly wondered if the shopping she'd just done would turn out to be unnecessary. Isabella had been a wonderful cook. The kitchen was sure to be well stocked. "I can do all that." She paused, bit her lip and even tried, unsuccessfully, to squeeze out a tear or two. "Poor Isabella had no relatives, as far as I'm aware. So once the police have finished with their investigations, I'm going to have to go through all her things."

"She had some lovely stuff," Gavin said. "I guess most of it will be good enough to go to charity."

"Yes, that's right. That sort of thing." *Charity my foot*, she thought. Isabella's clothes were going on Vinted, and she'd already arranged for one of the local auction houses to come and look at the furniture – the pieces she didn't want to keep for herself, that was. And as most of the furniture had been her mum's in the first place, it was hers to do with as she chose.

Penny declined Gavin's offer to make her coffee. So the young man headed back upstairs to finish packing. She looked around the cottage, trying to see it through others' eyes. The decor was a bit tired and frankly out of date. Her mother had done very little to the place in recent years, and Isabella had obviously been too busy. If she was going to get top dollar when she sold it, she'd need to have some work done.

She sat in one of the deep chintz-covered chairs in the sitting room and looked around with a pang of regret. This could be a wonderful place to live. If only she didn't need the money for her operation, she could live here very happily.

Then she sat up suddenly as a thought hit her. She did some sums in her head. Maybe if she sold all Isabella's personal effects, plus a few bits of furniture. And of course, there was Isabella's car. That would fetch a bit more. Then she could get a lodger. One who'd pay a proper rent this time. There was a large spare room upstairs. And she wouldn't mind sharing the kitchen just for a while.

Penny relaxed back against the chair and started to smile. It might just work. She looked a couple of years into the future. With her operation done and dusted, she could get rid of her tenant – better make sure the lease was watertight this time – and settle down very happily in her mother's cottage; her inheritance would finally be hers.

At that moment, her thoughts were disturbed by the sound of the front gate opening. Peering through the windows, she was surprised to see two complete strangers, a man and a woman, walking up the path. Jehovah's Witnesses, maybe. They certainly looked smart enough.

"Yes, can I help you?" she said, opening the front door. The man spoke as they both pulled wallets out of their pockets and flashed their IDs at her.

"I'm DS Smith, this is DC Wellman. We're looking for Mr Porter. Is he in? We'd like a word with him."

CHAPTER 35

When the police heard Penny was the owner of Isabella's cottage, they'd spent time chatting to her before asking again for Gavin. Calling him downstairs and introducing the two detectives, she'd suggested they use the lounge to talk. She closed the door to give them – and her – some privacy and then headed into the kitchen. Glancing at the clock, she tutted. Nearly six. Neil would be wondering where she was. She pulled her mobile from her pocket and hit the top number in her frequent calls list.

"Hello, it's me. Yes, I'm sorry. There's been a lot going on here. No, nothing I can't handle. Just had the cops round. In fact they're still here. What? Why do you think? They're looking for Isabella's killer. No, no idea by the look of it. But they're talking to that young lodger of hers now. And I reckon he's got something to hide. Shifty young thing, he is. Welsh. Never liked the Welsh!"

She closed her eyes as a torrent of words came down the phone at her. While Neil continued to talk, Penny closed her eyes and drifted off, thinking about the plan forming in her mind since she'd sat in the lounge this afternoon and dared to think about a future on her own terms. But she needed to take things slowly if she was going to get away with it.

Realising with a start she was now listening to silence, she opened her eyes and smiled broadly. Someone had once told her a smile could be 'heard' at the other end of the phone and although she wasn't sure it was true, she always thought it was worth a try.

"Look, Neil, I know it's a bit lonely for you all on your own, but I need to stay here for the moment. And I think we can turn this whole situation to our advantage. Forget the original plan; I've got a much better idea. No, I don't want to go into details now. I'll tell you tomorrow. Don't wait up for me. I'll see you in the morning. Bye, Neil." And she disconnected the call before he could say anything else.

Penny Conway had been on a downward spiral when she met Neil Harding a few years back. Mourning the death of her long-term partner, she'd lost her job and her home. Standing on the top of Berry Head in Brixham, she'd been toying with the idea of ending it all, when someone had stopped beside her.

"It's never that bad, you know. There's always someone worse off than you."

Crippled with arthritis, Neil was on crutches at the time, but these days he was virtually housebound. He and Penny had met every day after that, and when he'd offered her lodging in return for a bit of help with the house and garden, she'd jumped at it. And he never asked for any rent, which was just as well, really. But these days, he was beginning to get a bit too clingy for her liking. She would always be grateful to him for the help he'd provided, but maybe it was time for a clean break. She'd been vague when he'd asked about her mother's cottage, and never mentioned the name of the village. So if she disappeared, he would not be able to find her. And this latest turn of events made that a lot more feasible than previously. Penny was sorry about Isabella and the nature of her death, but all in all, it looked as though things were looking up for her.

CHAPTER 36

Michael Henning had lived in Devon long enough to be used to the narrow winding lanes. But he still found the route to Henry's home difficult to follow, and the satnav was no help at all. Eventually, after a couple of wrong turnings, a near miss with a white van driver on a very steep hill, and several delays caused by cyclists riding two abreast, he pulled up at the wooden gates to Whitehead House. The high-tech box looked out of place on the gatepost, but when Michael pushed the button, he got an immediate response.

"Come on in, my boy. Drive right up to the house. You can park outside."

The gate swung open, and Michael drove through. The driveway was bordered on both sides by rhododendron bushes that grew to more than the height of a man. The surface was pitted with potholes. Michael guessed Henry didn't get too many visitors these days. But then the driveway widened, the bushes ended, and the house came into view. Michael slammed on the brakes and swerved to a halt, open-mouthed. It was magnificent. That was the only word for it. Built in soft grey, local stone, it was a two-storey building in the traditional E shape. The main front porch formed the centre of the E, while short wings at either end of the building stretched forward, in perfect symmetry. The windows consisted of small leaded panes supported by thick stone mullions. As Michael restarted the engine and drove closer to the building, he could see the panes were dull rather than sparkling, and the stonework looked weathered in the extreme, but this didn't detract from the initial impression.

He jumped out of the car and locked it, although he doubted if there was any crime risk this far into the Haldon Hills. But it was a habit he was unable to break. He wondered if he should go to the front porch. The heavy oak door looked way too imposing. But at that moment, Henry Whitehead appeared around the corner of the house, preceded by a small black and white ball of fur that threw itself at his knees.

"Hello, Bertie. So you remember me, do you?" The tiny body was positively quivering as Henry's Jack Russell tried to reach Michael's fingers. He bent and scratched the dog behind his ears. Then he stood and held out his hand to his host.

"Hello, Henry. What a magnificent house."

Henry smiled and nodded, looking up at the building behind them.

"Yes, it's beautiful, isn't it? You can see why I want to preserve the family name, can't you?"

"Oh, definitely." Michael paused as the two men basked in the magnificence around them. "But isn't it very big for one person?"

"I'm afraid you've hit the nail on the head, Michael. And it costs a bomb to maintain, although it's worth every penny, and Great-great-great-uncle Aubrey's legacy means money's not an issue." Henry sighed. "In fact, as you'll see, I only use a tiny part of the place. And after I'm gone…" He shook his head and shrugged. Then he smiled. "But let's not think about all that now. Come on, let's go and get a coffee and you can tell me how it went on Saturday afternoon."

Henry led the way around the back of the house and in through a much smaller door than the impressive entrance at the front. They walked down a narrow passageway panelled in dark oak, and into a surprisingly bright and modern kitchen. Henry turned to Michael as he filled the kettle. "As you can see, not everything in this house is rooted in the Middle Ages. My parents did very little to the place, and we still had gas lights until the 1970s. But when I inherited, I had the electricity put in and this part of the house modernised. I've got this small living area and pretty much spend all my time down here. We used to have lots of visitors when I was a child but these days, it's just me and Bertie on our own most of the time." He placed a cafetière on a tray with delicate china mugs and a plate of biscuits, and led the way into a book-lined study. There was a stone fireplace at one end in which logs were burning brightly.

"I know it's warming up out there," he said, "but this house always takes a while to catch up with the weather, so I keep a fire burning in here most of the year." He gestured to a deep maroon leather chesterfield chair to one side of the fireplace. "Do sit down, Michael." He sank into an identical chair opposite his guest. "We'll have a coffee and then you talk me through those changes you mentioned." Michael had already spotted the gleaming baby grand in the corner and was itching to have a go at it. He suspected Henry kept it in as good a condition as his library and his kitchen. Whatever the state of the rest of the house, Henry Whitehead appeared to be fastidious about his immediate living quarters and prized possessions.

Coffee drunk, Michael picked up his score and approached the piano. He lifted the lid, propped open the top to an approving nod from Henry, and ran his fingers gently along the keys. The tone was like honey and perfectly tuned. Michael sat down, opened his score, and began to play. Henry closed his eyes, leaned back in his chair and steepled his fingers. His toe tapped gently on the floor in time to the beat.

As Michael finished playing, there was a moment of pure silence before Henry opened his eyes and slowly clapped his hands.

"Oh well done, my boy," he said. "You've made a wonderful job of that. The changes are quite subtle, but they'll make all the difference to that final scene." He paused, putting one bony forefinger to his lips and then continued. "If I might make just a couple of suggestions?"

His 'couple of suggestions' turned out to be a list of about a dozen changes, most of which were minor and relating to the libretto. Michael had no problem with those. But when Henry suggested resetting one passage in a totally different key, he felt his hackles rise. Was the sponsor of the production attempting to tell his musical director how to amend his composition?

"I have to disagree, Henry." He could feel his smile freezing on his face but was unable to stop himself from continuing. "That passage is perfect just as it is." He held up his hand as Henry opened his mouth to argue. "No, Henry, I'm sorry. I fully accept this is a collaborative project. And I'm happy to defer to you on the words and the staging. But you really have to understand the music is my department. As it was Isabella's."

"Yes, yes, of course, my boy." Henry stood up, the warmth of his flush spreading to his neck and his ears. "I quite understand. Forgive me." He gathered the empty mugs and put them on the tray, before pulling an ornate fob watch out of his pocket. Michael stopped gathering his notes together and pointed at the timepiece.

"That's a nice specimen? Family heirloom, is it?"

"It certainly is, my boy. Great-great-great-uncle Aubrey brought it back from the East Indies as a matter of fact. It was a present from him to his nephew, my great-grandfather. It's been handed down through the generations ever since."

"Mind if I take a look?"

"Do you know a bit about watches then?"

"As a matter of fact, I do. My father was a collector and he taught me quite a bit about them." Michael examined the piece then handed it back to Henry with a smile. "Nice to see a real old-fashioned watch for a change. Everyone seems to use their phones to tell the time these days."

"Indeed." There was a slight pause. "Right, I'm sure you've got a busy day ahead of you, so I'll show you out now."

The two men shook hands outside the impressive front entrance. As Michael drove away, he pondered on Henry's attempt to interfere with the music. And he wondered if Isabella had experienced the same issues? But one thing he did know. There was no way he'd accept interference from Henry Whitehead – or anyone else – when it came to his compositions. He'd done that once before and look where it had got him.

CHAPTER 37

Michael pushed his chair back from the keyboard and gave a deep sigh of relief and pleasure. He'd made great progress and was now completely happy with the music for *The Hero's Return*. And the changes were so minor, subtle, as Henry had called them, that he was sure the musicians would have no difficulty taking them on. He was pretty sure Henry would be pleased with the outcome, despite not getting his way on that key change. And he'd managed to talk him out of the daft idea of a walking ending and fireworks on the green. The singers and musicians would thank him for that. His suggestion of a party in the garden of The Falls to which all the audience would be invited seemed to have gone down well. He glanced at his phone to check the time. That reminded him. There was something he wanted to look up before he phoned Henry with an update. Something had been niggling him since he'd visited Henry that morning. Michael's father had been a keen horologist and the interest had rubbed off on him. He was pretty sure he'd be able to find out what he was looking for in one of the old man's books up in the spare room.

Two hours, several books and a long session on Google later, Michael had his answer. Henry described his fob watch as being gifted to his great-grandfather by Great-

great-great-uncle Aubrey. And he seemed to think it had been made in the East Indies in the early nineteenth century. But Michael suspected it was at least a hundred years older than that. If he was correct, it was European in origin, from Germany or France. Which meant it was even more valuable than Henry realised. And it could be a great talking point in the promotion Henry was doing for *The Hero's Return*. And a positive story was just what they needed after the recent tragic events.

Michael reached for his phone.

"Henry, it's Michael. Didn't disturb you, did I?"

"No, no, of course not, my boy. I've just got in from walking Bertie. What can I do for you? How are you getting on?"

"Not bad. Not bad at all, Henry. I think you'll be pleased with the final changes I've made. But I've got something else I want to discuss with you. Something that might help you build your family's reputation even more than this production will. It's about that watch of yours. I've been doing a bit of research and I think it might be even older than you think. And therefore, much more valuable."

There was a pause. Henry cleared his throat.

"That sounds interesting, Michael. What have you learned?"

"Well, it's only a thought at the moment…" Michael broke off. He didn't want to make a fool of himself. Maybe he'd got hold of the wrong end of the stick. "Look, I tell you what, Henry. You're coming on the hike on Sunday, aren't you?"

"Oh yes, of course I am. I love a ramble across the moors, and it'll do Bertie good to have a proper run."

"Fair enough. Well, let me do some more research over the next few days, and then we'll walk together on Sunday, and I'll talk you through my ideas then. How does that sound?"

"It sounds perfect, my boy. I'll see you on Sunday. Hounds Tor car park, isn't it?"

"That's right. Ten o'clock start. See you then. Goodnight, Henry."

"Good night, Michael. Sweet dreams."

CHAPTER 38

Gavin heaved his bag onto the bed and looked out of the window across the car park and up into the Haldon Hills. What a week! Losing Isabella – and in such a violent way. Resigning from his first major role – he was pretty sure that had been the right decision, but his stomach lurched every time he thought about what he'd done. Packing up at the cottage, with the intention of heading back to Wales.

It had been a shock when the two detectives had arrived the afternoon before. He'd heard the car arrive and, watching from the bedroom window, he'd seen two strangers walk up the path. He'd assumed they were friends of Penny. They certainly seemed to be spending quite a bit of time talking to her. Then she'd called him down, introduced him to DS Smith and DC Wellman, and left them to it.

Once he'd got over the shock, the interview, if you could call it that, was pretty straightforward. Yes, Isabella had been his landlady, so he'd spent quite a bit of time with her. Yes, they got on very well – just how well, he kept to himself. No, he couldn't think of anyone who would want to attack her. She was very popular in the village; everyone seemed really upset at the news of her death. Where had he been on the evening of Sunday 26th March? Alone in the cottage, all evening. He'd had a heavy week of rehearsals and his voice was suffering a bit, so he'd gone to bed early. No, he hadn't worried when Isabella hadn't come home. He assumed she'd gone for a drink with some of the choir. It was only in the morning that he'd realised she wasn't there.

He didn't think they suspected him of having a hand in Isabella's death. In fact, he wasn't sure they even knew about his relationship with the dead woman, so he'd been a bit taken aback when they said he wasn't to leave the village for the time being. He was beginning to think he was cursed and would never get out of Coombesford.

Having told Penny earlier on the Sunday that he would leave the cottage as soon as possible, he'd walked across to The Falls, and had been relieved when Charlie told him they had a room free from today. He'd booked it for a week initially, and phoned his mum to say he wouldn't be coming home just yet after all. She'd been as disappointed as he was and the sound of her quiet voice trying to make the best of the situation had almost brought him to tears.

Now, he unpacked his clothes, pushed the empty bag on top of the wardrobe and looked around. Pale, slightly patterned wallpaper. A couple of nice pieces of vintage crockery on the old oak chest of drawers, and a good, wide comfortable-looking bed. A nice room, but a bit too claustrophobic for his mood. He decided he'd pop down to the bar and have a quick drink before going for a walk. He might even find himself a quiet spot and do a bit of outdoor vocal practice.

CHAPTER 39

"It's Penelope, isn't it? Penelope Conway?"

Penny looked up at the voice. The woman behind the bar grinned at her as she put a full pint glass in front of her.

"I'm Charlie Jones. We don't see you in here very often."

"Thanks, Charlie, and good to meet you. Yes, I'm Penelope Conway; Penny." She took a sip and licked her lips in appreciation. "No, I've not been here for ages. I live over Brixham way." She paused. "At least I do at the moment."

"Thinking of moving, are you?"

"Could well be, Charlie. Now the cottage is empty. You knew poor Isabella was my tenant, I assume?"

Charlie nodded.

"Yes, I'd heard that. Very sad business."

"Indeed." Penny let the conversation lapse for a moment or two, knowing she would be expected to show at least a modicum of regret for the way in which her cottage had become free. "How long have you been in Coombesford?"

"Only three years. I moved here with my partner, Annie, and our daughter. But we love it. Wouldn't want to live anywhere else."

"So you never met my mother? Isabella was her tenant

to start with."

"And you let her stay on after your mother's death. That's very generous of you."

"Hmm, yes, well. Some might say too generous." Penny took another drink, realising this was probably not a good time to badmouth her former tenant. "But that's as may be. The cottage is empty now and I have to decide what to do with it."

"Putting it up for sale, are you? It should fetch a good price, prime location like that, on the edge of the green."

Penny shrugged.

"Yes, that's what I thought. But you know what, Charlie, I'm not so sure now. I've spent quite a few hours there this past couple of days and it's a nice little place. Needs a bit of doing up, of course. But I may well decide to move in there myself."

"Well, if you do, I'm sure you'll enjoy village life as much as we do. Excuse me." Penny continued to muse over her plans for the future until Charlie returned from the other end of the bar where she'd been serving someone else.

"I couldn't help noticing the police came to the cottage yesterday afternoon," said Charlie. "Have they got any closer to finding out who killed Isabella?"

"Well, if they have, they weren't sharing it with me. They were there for young Gavin, but when they heard I was the owner of the cottage, they asked if they could talk to me too."

"What, formal-like? At the station?"

"Goodness, no. It was just a chat, to get some background on Isabella. Nice young couple of detectives, they were. The DS seemed to know what he was about. But the DC was very new to it all. Said it was her first murder investigation." Penny pulled a face. "To be honest, Charlie, I got the impression they were a bit out of their depth. We talked about Isabella and her tenancy. They wanted to know if I could suggest anyone who would want to harm her. But I said I barely knew the woman. She paid her rent on time

137

every month and apart from occasional discussions about upkeep, I never really talked to her."

"So there wasn't much you could tell them, was there?"

"No, nothing really. Of course, they asked me where I was on the Sunday night. But I told them, I was at home in Brixham, minding my own business. After that, they seemed to run out of things to ask me and went to talk to Gavin instead."

"And do you have a partner in Brixham, Penny?"

Penny wondered, just briefly, whether she was being chatted up. Then she remembered the look on Charlie's face when she mentioned her partner and their daughter. No, she was just imagining things. She shook her head.

"No, there's just me, Charlie. I share a house with someone, but we live separate lives." She paused. "Of course, if I do move into the cottage, I'm going to need some help with the bills, at least at first. So if you hear of anyone looking for digs, just bear me in mind, will you?"

CHAPTER 40

"To be quite honest with you, it's a relief she's gone." Gavin couldn't believe it when those words came out of his mouth. Although they were somewhat slurred, and he wasn't sure the woman across the bar from him had fully understood what he'd said. The quick drink had turned into several pints, a ploughman's supper, and several more pints. Gavin had never got around to taking a walk or doing any singing. Now, as the evening drew to a close, he was the last man standing, although swaying would probably be more accurate. He gave a little giggle to himself and then belched. "Oh, excuse me!"

"That's okay, Gavin. Better out than in," said Charlie, who was busy clearing up the bar now everyone else had gone home.

"I'm very grateful to you for taking me in, Charlie. I didn't want to stay at the cottage any longer. And now the police want me to hang around. Not sure how long for."

"Well, don't you worry, Gavin. The room's yours for as long as you need it." She paused then went on. "You said it was a relief Isabella's gone. What did you mean?"

"Well, I don't know if it was common knowledge or not, but Isabella was a bit more than my landlady."

"Not common knowledge, no. But there were some of

us who suspected."

"The thing is, she was a nice woman and all that. Quite a bit older than me of course. But she was definitely the one making all the moves. I tried to break it off a couple of times. But once it had happened... there was no going back." Gavin took another sip of his pint. "She was very forceful, you see. And I was afraid of losing my job." He paused again. "Although as it happens, that wasn't as bad as I'd expected it to be." He looked across at his new landlady. "Do you think I'm a terrible person, Charlie?"

"No, of course I don't. It was a bit daft getting involved with her in the first place, but your reaction's quite normal." Charlie put the cloths over the beer pumps and turned to the coffee machine. "Any idea why the police want you to hang around?"

"No idea at all, Charlie. I mean, it's not as though I was planning on leaving the country." He paused and gave a wry grin. "Okay, that's exactly what I was planning on doing, but Wales is only just up the road from here. And my parents' farm is well known. They'd be able to find me anytime they needed me."

"Do they know about your relationship with Isabella?"

"Not as far as I know. They didn't mention it. Why?"

"Well, you know what they say. Most murderers are known to their victims. And even if they don't know how close you really were, you were living in the same house as her. So maybe it's standard practice."

"They did ask me where I'd been on the evening in question."

"And what did you tell them?"

"The truth. I was in the cottage on my own all evening. I went to bed early and didn't realise Isabella was missing until the following morning."

"Well, there you are then. You've nothing to worry about. I'm sure they'll let you go home soon." Charlie picked up two mugs of coffee and put one down in front of Gavin. "Here, get that inside you. Your head will thank me in the morning. You seemed to be having quite a chat with Penny earlier on."

"Yes, that was odd. Having pretty much turned me out yesterday, talking about looking for a quick sale, she now appears to be thinking about doing the place up and moving in herself. So she wants a lodger to help pay the bills."

"She did mention that, yes. And she offered you the room back?"

"She did indeed."

"And you said?"

"I said no thanks. I'm going back to Wales as soon as the police are ready to let me go." He finished his coffee, pushed the mug across the bar towards Charlie and then got unsteadily off his stool. "One lesson I've learned from all this, Charlie. I'll not be moving in with an older woman again! Apart from my mum, that is."

CHAPTER 41

When Annie pulled in at five to ten on the Sunday morning, there was quite a crowd gathered in the car park below Hounds Tor. First-timers were chuckling at the name above the serving hatch on the Burger Van. The Hound of the Basket Meals had been a regular feature there for as long as most people could remember.

Michael Henning and Henry Whitehead had been the first to arrive, judging by the prime positions they'd taken, parking next to the road. Michael was leaning on the back bumper of his car, tying the laces on his trainers. Henry, who had an ancient rucksack on his back, was holding two water bottles in one hand and Bertie's lead in the other. The young terrier was sniffing the air excitedly, obviously looking forward to racing free across the short stubby grass.

Charlie had declined to take part in the day, assuring Annie she was perfectly happy to stay back and run The Falls on her own. "Most of our regulars will be clambering over the moors, and no doubt doing their Julie Andrews impressions," she'd said. "And if we do get a sudden rush, I'll give Rohan a call. Just make sure you come back with the first group, it's going to get busy in here this evening."

Their daughter, on the other hand, had jumped at the chance of a day out on Dartmoor, especially as her beloved

Melanie was going to be there too. Suzy seemed quite shy when they parked up and saw how many people were there. But Annie knew she wouldn't take long to come out of her shell. She guessed the main difficulty would be stopping her from talking too much and irritating some of the older members of the choir.

"Right everyone," called Michael, clapping his hands together for silence. "You should all be able to see a copy of the map I've sketched out. I thought we'd start by going straight up the side here. It'll only take ten to fifteen minutes to get to the top of the tor. We can have a quick break there and then head south towards location number 1. That's a much longer piece and should take us to lunchtime. After that, we'll stroll along the side of the lake to location number 2, then come back here via location number 3." He looked around expectantly. "How does that sound?"

"Yep." "Fine." "All good." The chorus of responses was fairly positive, as would be expected from a group who'd lived most of their lives on the edge of the moors.

"Sounds like an awful lot of walking," piped up one of the basses, a rather forlorn-looking older man who seemed highly uncomfortable in his tight-fitting shorts and tee-shirt. There was a small titter of laughter, but several of the other older members nodded in agreement.

"Don't worry, Fred," said Michael. "I know you're not all experienced walkers. There's a much shorter route back you can take from the lunch site. I'll make sure there's someone to guide you."

Fred smiled and nodded.

"Much appreciated, Michael."

"Right then, are we all ready? Let's make a move."

Michael and Henry strode off across the road and everyone else formed a loose crocodile behind them. By the time the two men had reached the top of the slope, the group was spread out widely across the side of the tor. Annie could see this walk was going to take some people much longer than others.

"Come on, Suzy," she said, "let's get a move on. Melanie's way ahead of us." The two put on a spurt and started passing some of their companions quite quickly. But just before they reached the top, there was a squeal, followed by a shout and a groan. Annie looked up just in time to see Melanie spreadeagled on the ground.

"Mel," yelled Suzy, streaking up the rest of the slope, "what happened?"

By the time Annie reached them, Melanie was sitting up, but grasping her ankle and biting her lip in pain. She was as white as a sheet. As was Suzy. Melanie looked up and grimaced.

"Stupid me! I caught my foot in a rabbit hole and ended up on my face." She patted Suzy's arm. "It's okay, poppet, don't look so frightened. I'm not badly hurt. Just winded." She looked up at Annie and shook her head. "But I think I might have sprained this. I don't think I'm going to be able to go any further." She looked around and pointed at a brightly coloured water bottle that had bounced over the edge and come to rest halfway down the slope. "Could someone fetch that for me please? I'm sorry to be a pain." One of the younger tenors nodded and raced off.

"Here, have some of this in the meantime," said Michael Henning. Melanie took the bottle from his outstretched hand and raised it to her lips.

"Thanks, Michael, I needed that." She held it out to him, just as the tenor returned with her own bottle, which was covered in mud and possibly worse. Michael shook his head and gestured for her to keep it. Smiling her thanks, she took a deep breath and looked up at Annie. "Right, could you and Suzy help me up so I can check what the damage is?"

"Of course. And if it looks too bad, I'll drive you home." Annie wrapped an arm around Melanie's shoulders while Suzy took hold of her arm. Gently they lifted her to her feet. "How does that feel?"

"Not too bad, actually. Perhaps if I just wait for a while, I may be able to walk it off." She suddenly blinked rapidly and staggered slightly, leaning heavily on Suzy in the process. "Whoa, that doesn't feel right." She put her hand to her head. "I've gone all dizzy."

"Come on, sit on this rock," said Annie. "Are you sure you didn't bang your head when you fell?"

"Positive. But I really don't feel too good at all." Annie grabbed her phone and hit 999.

By this time, everyone was aware something was going on and there was quite a crowd gathered on the side of the hill.

"Okay, everyone," called out Annie. "Stand back please. Give her some room." She looked around for Michael and Henry. "I've called the emergency services. But there's no reason for everyone to wait around. Michael, Henry, why don't you carry on with the walk. Suzy and I will wait here with Melanie."

In the end, Michael agreed to take the walkers on, while Henry waited with Melanie and her two friends. As one of the two organisers of the day, he said he felt responsible for everyone's safety.

There was no sign of an ambulance, but to everyone's relief, a Dartmoor Ranger's Land Rover pulled up shortly afterwards with a trained first aider at the wheel. They transferred Melanie to the back seat, then Annie and Suzy jumped in their car. The two vehicles sped off across the moors in a convoy, leaving Henry to rejoin the walk, and arrived within forty minutes at Torbay A&E department.

Annie couldn't hear what the driver said to the medical staff but within minutes, Melanie was on a trolley and being wheeled inside. She paused to thank the driver before taking Suzy's hand and rushing inside. He smiled and shook his head.

"All part of the job." He paused. "I shouldn't be saying this to you really. And you'll have to wait for the results of the tests to be sure. But it doesn't look to me like your friend's suffering the after-effects of a fall. It looks more like something she's eaten has disagreed with her."

CHAPTER 42

It was rather a subdued group that gathered in The Falls late that afternoon. Annie had brought them up to date on Melanie's condition. She seemed to be recovering well and although she was being kept in overnight for observation, the medical staff didn't think there was anything major wrong with her. Charlie had phoned Edward and convinced him it wasn't necessary to cancel his concert that night. The tenor had promised to travel down to Devon early the next day.

The only thing Annie hadn't mentioned to anyone yet was the Ranger's suspicion that Melanie had been affected by something other than her fall. The general impression among those who'd seen the incident at Hounds Tor was that she must have hit her head when she fell and that the dizziness was a delayed reaction. Annie guessed they'd know the truth sooner or later, but decided it wasn't her role to spread rumours in advance.

"Anyone hungry?" called Charlie from behind the bar. Everyone looked her way and there was a chorus of assent. "Well, if you care to stroll into the restaurant, you'll find supper ready for you." She pointed around the corner and there was a general rush to follow her suggestion.

At one end of the room, a couple of tables had been

pulled together and covered with gleaming white cloths. Plates were piled high with sandwiches and sausage rolls, mini quiches, and slices of pork pie. A huge bowl of fresh fruit separated the savouries from delicate slices of brownies and tiny scones topped with clotted cream and strawberry jam.

"Wow. What a feast. Thank you, Annie," said Henry Whitehead as he led the procession to the table. For once, he had both hands free, and Annie guessed he'd left Bertie curled up in front of the fire in the bar. "You must've been up really early to get this lot prepared before you came out today?"

"Not me, Henry." Annie shook her head. "Not this time. It was all done while we were out. Charlie drafted in a couple of friends to help." At that point, Rohan and Esther appeared around the corner from the kitchen, holding the last couple of plates. "And here they are now. A round of applause, folks, for Charlie and the gang."

There was the sound of hand clapping and a few cheers, but silence soon descended as the hungry walkers made short work of the food. Annie winked at her friends, then took her loaded plate back into the bar to chat to Henry and Michael, who'd bagged the best table next to the fire. As expected, Bertie was curled up at their feet.

"Can I join you, gents?" she said, pulling out a chair and dropping into it. "Phew, what a day." She grinned ruefully at them. "Not exactly how we expected it to turn out!"

"Indeed no," said Henry. "I'd have come with you, Annie, but that Ranger was adamant it wasn't necessary."

"Well, no, that's right. And you couldn't have brought Bertie into the hospital anyway." At the sound of his name, the young Jack Russell opened an eye and lazily wagged his tail. "Yes, I'm talking about you," she said, reaching down and scratching behind his ears.

"Annie, I'm so sorry," said Michael, coming out of a daze with a start. "You don't have a drink. Let me go and get you one."

"No, no, thank you, Michael." She realised her words might have sounded a tad sharper than she intended them. But somehow, after what had happened to Melanie, she didn't want to take a drink from anyone, especially not Michael. To her relief, Charlie appeared at her elbow at that moment and popped a mug down in front of her. She smiled her thanks and turned back to her companions. "As you can see, Charlie knows me so well. I'll take one of her hot chocolate specials over anything else any day. Especially after a day walking on the moors."

"Or not, as the case may be," said Henry with a smile.

"Indeed."

At that moment, the door from the car park flew open and everyone stopped talking. DS Derek Smith strode into the room, followed by a smartly-dressed young woman Annie didn't recognise, but assumed was another detective. The young woman flushed bright red at being the centre of attention, and rapidly scurried towards the bar with her sergeant. Charlie walked to meet them, and the level of noise rose once more as everyone else started talking – or at least pretended to. Annie saw Charlie point over in the direction of their table. Her heart sank. Surely not. It couldn't be bad news, could it? Melanie had been recovering well when she left her a couple of hours ago. But it wasn't her the pair had come to see.

"Mr Henning? Mr Michael Henning?"

Michael jumped as though he'd been shot.

"Yes, that's me. What can I do to help you?"

"I'm DS Smith and this is DC Wellman. We'd like you to come into Exeter with us, Mr Henning. We need to talk to you."

"What, now?" Michael looked at his watch. "It's getting late, and it's been a long day. Can't it wait until tomorrow?"

DS Smith shook his head.

"No, sorry, sir, but it can't wait. We need a chat this evening. Now, in fact. There's a car outside."

"Oh, very well." Michael pulled a face and standing,

grabbed his coat. "I'll need to phone my kids and tell them where I'm going."

"You can do that from the car, sir." DC Wellman took him gently but firmly by the arm and steered him towards the door.

By now, the bar had gone silent again as everyone gave up any pretence of minding their own business. The silence persisted as the door banged shut behind them, an engine fired, and the police car drove away. Only then did the talking start up once again. Annie kept silent, and looked meaningfully across the bar to where the other three members of the Gang of Four were quietly chatting. She had a good idea what that was all about. Time for another meeting, maybe.

CHAPTER 43

"Sit down, Mr Henning. Thank you for agreeing to come in for this chat at such short notice." Joanne Wellman tried to make it sound as though the man in front of her was there voluntarily. But she knew he wasn't really. And she knew he knew it too. As his words confirmed.

"Well, I didn't have much choice in the matter, now did I?"

"Can we get you anything to drink? Coffee? Tea?"

"No, nothing thank you." Michael Henning looked pointedly at his watch. "Let's just get on with it, shall we? I take it this is to do with Isabella's death?"

"Possibly, yes, but maybe not." The two detectives sat down at the table opposite him. "What we want to talk about at the moment is the incident on the moor today."

"Incident? What incident?" Michael wrinkled his forehead.

"The collapse of Ms Melanie Unwin."

"Oh, that. Well, I wouldn't call it an incident, more of an accident really. She caught her foot in a rabbit hole, fell heavily and twisted her ankle. She was shaken up but fine otherwise to start with. Then she started feeling dizzy, which was when we called for the Rescue people." He stopped and raised an eyebrow at the couple opposite him. "But you guys are on the murder team. Why are you interested in a minor accident on Dartmoor?"

"We'll come to that, Mr Henning," DS Smith broke in. "Could you just talk us through the incident as you remember it?"

"Well, it all seems a lot of fuss about nothing, but if it'll help me get out of here before midnight, here goes. I was at the head of the group with Henry and Bertie…"

"That's Henry Whitehead, is it, sir?"

"Yes, that's right. We were chatting about the plans for the day, when we heard a scream. When we turned round, poor Melanie was flat on her face a few yards behind us. So we ran back to help her."

"And what did you do?"

"We lifted her up and sat her on one of the rocks. At that point Annie McLeod arrived with her young daughter and took control."

"Why was that, do you think, sir?"

"Well they're good friends, I believe. Melanie is one of young Suzy's childcare team."

"And what happened next, Mr Henning?"

"Um, let me think. Oh yes, Melanie had dropped her water bottle and it rolled down the slope. She asked one of the guys to fetch it for her, but in the meantime, I gave her my own bottle."

"And did she give it back to you?"

"No, I told her to keep it. Hers had ended up in a muddy puddle and wasn't fit to use."

"Did anyone else have access to your bottle this morning, Mr Henning?"

"No, I don't think so. My son filled it for me while I was getting ready to leave home."

"And how do you get on with your sons, sir?" asked Derek Smith.

"As well as any father gets on with teenagers who only live with him half the time and are a dab hand at playing one parent off against another." He looked from one detective to the other, clear signs of agitation on his face. "Look what is this all about? Why are you so interested in my water bottle? You don't think there was something wrong with the contents, do you?"

"We're just trying to look at all aspects of the incident, sir."

Joanne Wellman placed a plastic evidence bag in the middle of the table. It contained a black rubber-covered water bottle.

"Can you confirm this is your water bottle, Mr Henning?"

Michael glanced at the bottle and nodded his head. Then he stopped and looked again, picking up the bag for a closer look.

"No. It's not. My bottle has an orange band around the bottom. This one's red."

"You're certain about that?"

"Absolutely, yes." He thought for a moment, then clicked his fingers. "That's it. In the car park this morning, just before we started out. I gave my bottle to Henry to hold while I retied one of my laces. He was juggling my bottle, his and Bertie's lead all at the same time. He must have given me his by mistake."

Joanne Wellman and Derek Smith exchanged a look before the DS turned to Michael with a smile.

"Okay, Mr Henning. I think that's all we need to ask. Thank you for your time. We'll get someone to run you home."

"So it looks like Michael Henning wasn't the target after all," said Joanne Wellman after they'd watched their interviewee follow a police driver across the foyer and out of the front door. Derek Smith nodded.

"Yes. And if Henry Whitehead's in the killer's sights, it's more than likely to be connected to this opera thing." He checked his watch. "Look, it's way too late to contact him now. Let's get some shut-eye and start again in the morning. We'll pop in and see him, just to give him a warning.

Although until we get the toxicology results, this is all speculation."

"True. Melanie Unwin's attack could be completely unrelated to that water bottle. But I don't really believe that, Sarge."

"No, Jo. Neither do I."

CHAPTER 44

"Right, let's make a start. What have we learned so far?" Rohan looked around the table at his three friends or the rest of the Gang of Four as Annie insisted on calling them. "Annie, you start."

Annie ran her fingers through her bright pink hair and blew her fringe out of her eyes.

"Not sure I've found out very much, to be honest. I've chatted to most of the chorus members, but no-one could tell me anything. They aren't all in the church choir, of course, so some of them weren't even in Coombesford that Sunday evening. And the ones that were there headed off to the pub in a group. I've checked that with several of them and they all say the same thing. They left together, arrived at The Falls together, and no-one went off on their own until they left around ten pm."

"And the police think she was killed around eight," said Rohan, "so that puts them in the clear."

"Yes, I remember that crowd," said Charlie. "They were wondering where Henry was. And just then, he phoned. Said his dog Bertie wasn't well, so he'd stayed at home with him for once. Some of the singers offered to go up to the house in case he needed help, but he said it wasn't necessary. He was going to keep an eye on him and call the vet if he was no better in the morning. But the little fellow was fine by the next evening, so it must have been something he ate."

"Of course, the only one who didn't go to the pub was Melanie," Annie continued. "She went back to the cottage and spent the evening alone. So she doesn't have an alibi, I'm afraid."

"But neither does Gavin Porter," said Charlie. "We were chatting last week, and he told me he spent the whole of the evening at Isabella's. Said he didn't go out at all."

"Well, I don't think that's true!" Annie shuffled through her notebook. "Look, I'm right. Melanie bumped into him outside the church as she was leaving. Literally bumped into him in fact, she ended up in the hedge. She only mentioned it because she thought he was acting a bit furtively. Said he was waiting for someone, but then disappeared in the direction of the village green and she didn't see him again."

"Interesting." Rohan glanced at Esther, but she was way ahead of him and was already writing 'Gavin – alibi' on the flip chart. "Anything more, Charlie?"

"Well, I also had a long chat with that woman who owns Isabella's cottage."

"Penelope Conway?" asked Annie.

"Yes, that's right. The one with all the tattoos. It looks like she's going to be moving into the cottage herself."

"But I thought Gavin said she was selling it? That's why he moved in with you guys, isn't it?" said Rohan.

Charlie nodded.

"Yes, that was the original plan. But by last Monday night she'd changed her mind. She's talking about doing it up and giving up her place in Brixham."

"She'll liven up the village," said Annie with a giggle.

"Well, yes, someone in the pub the other night mentioned hearing a terrific row between her and Isabella a few days before the murder. Apparently Penny was going out of the front gate and Isabella was screaming at her, something about Penny getting the cottage over her dead body."

There was a shocked silence around the table and Rohan was sure he wasn't the only one who felt a shiver run through him.

"I wonder where she was on the night of Sunday 26th March," mused Annie.

"Well," said Charlie, "she assured me she was miles away from here, in Brixham. But by her own admission, she lives alone, so I guess she's another one with no alibi."

By now the list on the flip chart had grown. Gavin, Penny, and Melanie were all shown as having no alibi. And Gavin was known to have lied about his whereabouts.

"What about Michael?" asked Annie. "Has anyone talked to him? Do we know anything about his whereabouts?"

"But he didn't appear on the scene until the night of the wake," said Esther. "Why would we need to think about him?"

"I'm not sure that's necessarily true," said Charlie. "He obviously knew quite a bit about *The Hero's Return* before he got involved. And Henry told me the other night Michael had been in Coombesford at least once before, listening to one of the rehearsals."

There was a pause, and everyone turned to look at Rohan.

"We're not getting very far, are we?" he said. "Right, time for some new assignments, I think." He started ticking off on his fingers. "Charlie and Annie, you try and find out why Gavin lied. And where he really was on the Sunday evening. Also, is Penelope Conway still around?"

Annie nodded.

"Yes, she's staying at the cottage for a couple more days, I think."

"Well, why don't you see if you can find out a bit more about her?"

"Sure. I'll pop in later and see if she needs any help."

"And Esther and I see what we can find out about Michael Henning." He glanced at the cuckoo clock over the fireplace. "Right, I'm supposed to be helping Celia in the café this lunchtime. I'll see you guys later."

CHAPTER 45

Esther hummed to herself as she scrolled through the archives for Newcastle University. Looking through the graduation lists for the early 2000s, she'd found Isabella Street quite easily. According to Annie, Isabella had studied English up on Tyneside, and sure enough, there she was at the top of the list for 2003. A first-class honours degree, no less.

Michael Henning had been quite quiet about his background, other than saying he and Isabella went way back. Esther had trawled through all the departments for that year, and for the year either side. With no result. She was about to give up and try another approach, when she spotted a list of societies on the website, including Music Soc. And there she found what she was looking for. Michael Henning, a postgraduate student, three years older than Isabella. When she returned to the graduation list for 2001, there he was, graduating with a Master's in Music. And with a special mention for having the best dissertation piece of his year.

Once she knew where to look, the rest was easy. Back copies of the college magazines had articles about the talented young musician who was off to Vienna to make a name for himself. And in several pictures of social events that summer, she spotted a young Michael Henning with his arm unmistakably wrapped around a young Isabella Street. So it was clear that at least for a time, Michael and Isabella were a couple. What had gone wrong, Esther wondered? And would there be anyone still around who might remember?

She pulled up the staff list for the current faculty, along with their photos. The Head of Department for Music was a smartly-dressed woman who looked to be in her late fifties. Her CV showed she'd been on the staff, albeit in more junior positions, for the past twenty-five years. Which meant she'd have been in post when Michael Henning was a student.

Esther grabbed her phone and called Rohan.

"Hi, Esther, what can I do for you?"

"Rohan, do you fancy doing a quick interview with someone at Newcastle University?"

"I could do. But it's a long way to go for just a short time. How about you give me the details and I'll see if I can sort it out over Zoom?"

"Brilliant idea. And much cheaper too. Here's what I'd like you to do."

A couple of hours later, a sharp rap on the back door told Esther she had a visitor.

"Only me. Can I come in?"

"Of course you can, Rohan. And this is going to be your home from next week. You really don't need to knock every time you arrive."

"Okay." The young man grinned at her. "I'll try to remember." He opened his eyes wide and looked winsome. "Is the kettle boiled by any chance?"

"Yes, it is. Sit down and tell me your news while I make the coffee." She paused and grinned at him. "But once you are a lodger, rather than a visitor, you're going to have to start making the coffee yourself sometimes."

Within moments the two were seated either side of the

fireplace with coffee and cookies – lemon butter this time. Esther could see Rohan was bursting to bring her up to date. She took a sip of coffee and nodded for him to start.

"The professor was extremely helpful. Said she remembered Michael Henning very well. He was one of her first postgrad students when she joined the faculty. She said he was a nice young man, polite and hardworking, always got his assignments done on time. He won the prize for the best music composition in his year. And everyone was delighted to hear he'd got the job in Vienna." Rohan paused to take a bite from one of the cookies and to murmur his appreciation before continuing. "She told me how disappointed she was when the job in Austria turned sour."

"Turned sour? Was that the phrase she used?"

"It was indeed. Apparently, she had a good friend in the same orchestra in Vienna, who told her there'd been a huge row between Henning and the musical director. Something about Henning not getting a role he was expecting. So he resigned. He travelled around Europe for a few years, singing minor roles, but in the end he gave up and came home to England. She never heard from him again after that."

"How sad. Seems like he had a promising career."

"That's right. According to her friend, the musical director in Vienna was going to give him the next major role that came along and had high hopes for him. But Henning was just too impatient. The professor admitted the one thing she'd not liked about him was his tendency to flare up if he didn't get his own way."

"So it looks like our Michael Henning has a bit of a temper on him, then?"

"It does indeed. I think I'll warn Annie not to cross him when she's at rehearsals." He paused and closed his notebook. Then he reopened it and studied his notes once more. "I nearly forgot. There was one strange thing she said at the end of our call. Apparently, hard-working as Michael was, initially he was a fairly mediocre student. He got his place on the Master's course by the skin of his teeth. His singing was fine, but his composing was somewhat pedestrian, in her words."

"Hang on. You said he won the composition prize at the end of the year."

"That's right, he did. Apparently there was a major change in his work midway through the year. I asked her what she thought caused that and she said it happened around the time Michael got himself a girlfriend."

"Really? Now that's interesting. Do you think Isabella was that girlfriend?"

"I think she must have been. The dates certainly fit. Perhaps all he needed was a bit of inspiration."

"You mean Isabella was his muse?"

"Sounds like it."

Rohan appeared to be quite relaxed with that thought, but Esther wasn't buying it.

"Well, it's possible I suppose. But there is another explanation. Remember when you guys told me about the night Michael volunteered to take on the MD's role? Apparently he said something about knowing Isabella's work very well. Maybe they worked together on his compositions. Maybe she was the better composer."

Rohan slapped a hand on the table.

"You could be right. And maybe, the reason he's managed to pick up the music of *The Hero's Return* so well is because he already knew it."

Esther grinned at him and the two said in harmony:

"It's the music they worked on together for his dissertation!"

"Well," said Esther, "if Isabella was using their music without giving him any credit for it, how do you think that would make him feel?"

"Mad as hell, I'd imagine."

"But mad enough to kill?"

"Ah, that's the question, isn't it, Esther?" Rohan took another cookie and munched on it as Esther considered the implications of everything the two of them had discovered that day.

CHAPTER 46

"I'm really not happy about this idea, Annie," Charlie said for the third time. Annie looked across at Rohan and Esther and winked. Then she went and sat down beside her partner and wrapped her arm around the other woman's shoulders.

"Charlie, we've been through this several times. We've planned for every eventuality. Nothing could possibly go wrong."

"Annie, this is a man that may or may not have deliberately poisoned our friend."

"Yes, Charlie, I know."

"And worse still, he may have killed Isabella."

"Yes, Charlie, I know."

"And you're going to put yourself in a room with him, all alone?"

"No, Charlie, not all alone. You guys will be right there too. I'll be perfectly safe."

"But if he tries anything, we might not be quick enough. I might not be quick enough. Maybe someone else should do it…"

Annie stood up and put her hands on her hips.

"Charlie Jones, will you listen to yourself! How many times have you planned this sort of thing in the past? And how many times have you closed down my objections with assurances that everything will be fine? And weren't you always right?"

"Well, yes, most of the time. But I was trained…"

"And you've trained me over the years, Charlie. I'll be fine, honestly."

Charlie shrugged and gave a rueful grin.

"Alright, I give in. But remember, if he offers you anything to drink, just say no."

Annie smiled at her co-conspirators. As she turned away, she hoped they wouldn't spot the slight tremor in her hands or the way she'd had her fingers crossed when she swore nothing could go wrong. She was doing this for her friends. She was the only one of the four who could set up the meeting. But deep down, she really hoped Charlie had been worrying unnecessarily. She picked up her mobile.

"Hello, is that Michael? Great. Michael, it's Annie McLean from the Coombesford Choir." She listened and laughed softly. "Yes, that's right, the one with the pink hair." She nodded. "Yes, I'm looking forward to this evening's rehearsal, but I have a bit of a problem with a couple of the passages in the alto part. Could you spare me five minutes at the end of the rehearsal? What? No, no. They're just silly little points, and I don't want to waste everyone else's time with them. I'd rather we did it privately at the end. Would that be okay? It would? Brilliant. Thanks. See you later."

She disconnected the call and gave the thumbs up sign to the others.

"Okay, all set. He was pushing to discuss them during the rehearsal, but I think I've persuaded him not to do that. I'd better think of a couple of genuine questions, however, just in case he does ask me in front of the others."

She gathered her things together and stood up from the farmhouse kitchen table. Walking across to Esther, she gave her a quick hug. "Thanks for hosting us again, Esther, and for the wonderful cookies. I'll let you know how I get on." Waving to Rohan and beckoning for Charlie to follow her, she headed for the door. She sighed and pretended not to hear Charlie's parting comment to their friends: "I'm really not at all comfortable about this."

CHAPTER 47

The rehearsal went well. At just after half nine, Michael Henning sent everyone home. A couple of the basses announced they were heading to The Falls for a quick drink. Michael said he'd join them as soon as he'd cleared up. As she listened to his exchange, Annie glanced around the church, trying not to make it too obvious she was looking for someone. She couldn't spot her guardians, but trusted they were there. They'd probably slipped in during the confusion of everyone else leaving.

"Right, Annie, what can I do for you?" Michael's words roused her from her thoughts. "You said you had some issues with the music."

Annie took a last look around the seemingly empty church and crossed her fingers that she wasn't really alone with this man who might just be a murderer. Then she squared her shoulders and turned towards him. She was surprised to find him standing right behind her. How had he done that without her noticing? She took a couple of steps backwards and found herself pushed up against the rood screen.

"I'm sorry, Michael," she said in a soft voice, going into the script she'd prepared with the rest of the Gang of Four that morning. "I was just thinking of poor dear Isabella. I can't help remembering her every time we come into church." She pointed to the vestry door. "It was in there, you know. Where Melanie found her."

"Yes, of course." Michael nodded. "I didn't think. Maybe we should have held our rehearsals somewhere else for a while?" He paused and shook his head. "Poor Isabella."

"You used to be close, didn't you?"

"That's right. We lived together for a while when I was studying for my Master's. She was in the second year of her degree course."

"What happened?"

"Oh, the usual story. I went abroad; she stayed in Newcastle. We tried to stay together, but it didn't work. We drifted apart. I didn't see or hear from her until I bumped into her when she was doing that interview on Radio Devon. And then, to lose her again after only one meeting. So sad." He bit his lip and shook his head. Then, as though mentally shaking himself, he smiled at her. "But that's not what you stayed behind to talk about, was it, Annie?"

Annie ignored his attempt to change the subject.

"But it wasn't just the one meeting, was it, Michael? You saw Isabella here in Coombesford at least twice, including on the evening she was killed."

"What? What are you talking about?" He paused and then stepped forward slowly. "What exactly are you suggesting?"

Annie swallowed hard and sidled along the rood screen, trying to put more distance between them.

"In the bar, on the night you volunteered to help us, you said you'd visited Isabella during one of our rehearsals. But the night she was killed was Evensong. You couldn't have heard the music that night."

"No, I visited her several days earlier. During one of the rehearsals."

"But your car was spotted in the village on the night she was killed." She paused and raised an eyebrow, hoping it would make her seem more confident than she felt. "Or were you visiting another old friend in Coombesford that night?"

"Look, this is ridiculous. How do you know it was my car in the car park? A silver Ford Mondeo is hardly an uncommon model."

Annie felt a surge in her gut. Got him. Her bluff had worked. But if she pointed it out, was she just putting herself in more danger?

"I don't believe Ms McLean mentioned anything about the car park, did she?" Annie nearly keeled over at the quiet voice from the middle of the church. Rohan Banerjee stepped out from behind one of the pillars. Michael Henning looked wildly across at the side aisle. But Charlie stepped out there.

"Don't even think about it, Henning," she said with a growl.

Michael Henning threw back his head and let out a groan. Then he reached for a chair and slumped down into it.

"Okay, I admit it. I was here that night. I needed to talk with Isabella. We'd already argued on the phone, and I wanted a chance to have it out with her face to face."

"Have what out with her?"

"The music. The score for *The Hero's Return*. It's my dissertation piece. Isabella stole it. She was passing it off as her own."

"But why would Isabella do that? She didn't need to. She was a talented composer."

"Yes, I know she was. And, to be fair, she did have some input. But the whole thing was primarily mine. We worked on some of the more difficult passages together, that's all."

"And you didn't know she'd claimed it as her own?"

"Not until I came to that Tuesday night rehearsal." He turned back to Annie. "I listened to you all singing and realised why it sounded so familiar. I didn't stop to speak to Isabella. At the time I was just disappointed in her. But then

I got angry. I tried talking to her on the phone a couple of nights later, but she just laughed in my face and told me to 'do my worst'."

"What did you want her to do? Stop using the music? Own up?"

"No, nothing like that. All I really wanted was some recognition. Joint billing would have been fine. The day after the phone call, I was raging at the injustice of it all. But by the weekend, I'd calmed down and thought I would have another go at talking to Isabella, face to face this time."

"And you came to see her on that Sunday night?"

"That's right. Her cottage was empty, so I thought I'd just pop into the church on the off chance. She was just about to lock up, so I didn't stop long. We had a reasonably civil conversation and she admitted she'd been having second thoughts. She was thinking about giving me joint billing. I was there about ten minutes, fifteen tops. And then I left." He stopped and looked up at Annie, then at the other two in the aisle. "You have to believe me. Isabella Street was alive and perfectly healthy when I left her."

"Then I think you'd better tell that to the police," said Charlie, taking out her phone.

CHAPTER 48

The empty glass landed on the bar with a hollow thud.

"Same again, Len?" called Charlie from the other end where she was topping up the stock of mixers. She watched with a straight face as the elderly farmhand checked his watch, held it to his ear and shook it, then glanced at the clock behind the bar to double check. It was the same performance she'd watched every day since they'd opened The Falls three years ago.

"Yeah, go on then, Charlie, you've twisted my arm." When the refilled glass was back in front of him, Len took a deep draught, then looked around. "Annie not on duty today, then?" He'd taken quite a shine to her partner, had Len. But it didn't bother Charlie in the least.

"Yes, she'll be here in a while, Len. She's on the phone at the moment. I think she's arguing with Henry Whitehead about the colour of her hair – again. Do you know he wants her to dye it brown for the performance! Well, you can guess how she took to that suggestion!"

Len looked at her in a puzzled manner.

"Performance? What performance? Is Annie going on the stage?"

"Only for one night, thank goodness. It's this opera Isabella Street wrote, based on Henry Whitehead's famous ancestor. Surely you've heard about it? Annie's in the choir that's providing the backing to the main singers."

There was a grunt.

"We thought it would all be cancelled, what with Isabella's murder and all, but the choir was adamant they wanted to continue and Henry's delighted. And they found a friend of Isabella's to take over as musical director. But it's all a bit fraught, as you can imagine. There's only a couple more days to go." Charlie grabbed an envelope from behind the bar. "Here, Len, I've still got a few tickets. Why don't you take your Enid? It's going to be a great evening. We're even closing the pub for a couple of hours so I can take Suzy along."

Len took another drink. Then he put down his glass and shook his head.

"No thanks, Charlie. It's not my Enid's cup of tea. She prefers a bit of a sing-song, where she can join in. And frankly, you couldn't pay me to go and watch that. All a big lie, it is, after all!"

"A lie, Len? What do you mean?"

"Well, correct me if I'm wrong, Charlie, but isn't it the story of how Henry's ancestor came back from living abroad and became a big local benefactor?"

"Yes, that's right."

"Well, there you are, then. A lie, as I said."

Charlie put down the glass she'd been drying and walked over to where Len was sitting.

"I'm sorry, Len, I'm still lost."

The old man took a long pull at his pint. Putting his glass down, he patted the stool next to him.

"You'd better sit down, lass. This could take a while." He waited until Charlie, highly amused at being called a lass, came round to the front of the bar, and settled herself next to him, then he started talking again. "There're two very different versions of the Whitehead story. I'm surprised you've not come across them before."

Charlie shrugged.

171

"To be honest, Len, I'd never heard of the family until Annie started talking about this production, back at the start of the year. So assume I know nothing."

"Well, the official story is that old Aubrey Whitehead falls in love with a local girl, one of the servants at the big house. That the pair become inseparable, and nothing can pull them apart, see. And his parents are so upset about the thought of a scullery maid contaminating their precious family line, they ship their son off to the East Indies. There was even some talk that he was forcibly removed."

"Yes, there's a suggestion of that in *The Hero's Return*."

"But unbeknown to Aubrey, his sweetheart is in the family way. He disappears to the other side of the world, not knowing there's a kiddie on the way. And as you can imagine, life was so difficult in those days, and there weren't no National Health service or nothing of the like. And the young woman, Harmony her name was, she dies in childbirth. Her parents look after the babe, a little boy. They call him Aubrey after his dad."

Len took another drink.

"Anyway, time passes, and Aubrey Senior's parents get old. His father dies and his mother sends a message to Aubrey asking him to come home and take over running the estate, which is falling into disrepair and running out of money. It takes a while of course for the message to get across the seas, but months later, he arrives home. He's done really well for himself and has enough wealth to sort out the estate. So he's seen as a hero by the village and all the people who rely on the estate for a livelihood, you see."

Charlie nodded.

"Now Aubrey has never forgotten young Harmony and although he married while he was away, his wife's dead and he arrives home a widower with a young son, Carter, hoping to find his childhood sweetheart. When he hears she's died giving birth to their son, he declares he'll never remarry and vows to spend the rest of his life preserving her memory and looking after his two children."

"Well, it's all a bit Barbara Cartland for me, but I can see why Henry might want to revitalise the story." Charlie stood and went back behind the bar. "But you said there were two versions. Let me refill your glass and you can tell me the other one."

"Actually, it's not too different from the first one, apart from a couple of key points. Firstly, Aubrey might have fallen for Harmony, but she didn't reciprocate his feeling. In fact, I'm sorry to have to say that he probably forced himself on her. His parents certainly shipped him off to the East Indies, but she was glad to see him go. Then she found out she was expecting. She died in childbirth and her parents took the child in."

"Poor little mite. He didn't have much of a start in life, did he?"

"No, but although life was hard, his grandparents loved him and brought him up well. They never hid his origins from him. So the young boy grew into a man who hated his father and blamed him, quite rightly, for his mother's death."

"So that must have made for an interesting confrontation when Aubrey returned home. I take it he did return home?"

"Oh, yes, and he'd made his fortune overseas, so the bit about sorting out the estate was true. But Aubrey Junior told his father in no uncertain terms he'd make him pay for his mother's death. It must have been a terrific scene, as Aubrey Senior spent the rest of his days as a recluse, locked up in the house, afraid to venture out in case his son came after him." The old man shrugged. "So you can see, Charlie, there are two very different views of the Whitehead family ancestors."

"I can indeed, Len. But what makes you so sure the second story's true, rather than the first one? It could all be a vicious rumour."

"Well, it was my old dad that told me both stories when I was a nipper. He was a gardener, see, up at Whitehead

House. And one day he was working in the vegetable garden when he heard Mr Henry's father Anthony and his brother Crispin talking. Crispin was boasting about his Great-great-grandfather Aubrey and his son Carter, and how they'd saved the estate. Anthony was mocking him and telling him there were things he didn't know about his ancestors. And how Carter wasn't really the heir after all, as there was another son who was older than him. But Crispin said he did know, but it didn't make any difference. She was only a maid, and the older son was a bastard – begging your pardon, Charlie. And the survival of the family was far more important."

Len looked at his watch and swallowed the rest of his pint in one go. "Well, I can't sit here chatting all evening. My Enid will be wondering where I am."

"Interesting chat, Len, thanks. So the true story was certainly known by Henry's father. I wonder if Henry knows?"

"He may well do; but if he does, he's kept very quiet about it. I've known Henry Whitehead all my life and he's never had anything but good things to say about his Great-great-great-uncle Aubrey."

CHAPTER 49

Esther took a sip of coffee and a bite from one of her gingerbread cookies. She flexed her fingers like a pianist preparing to perform on stage, and attacked her keyboard.

"Right, Great-great-great-uncle Aubrey. Let's see what secrets you're hiding, shall we?"

Two hours slipped by as she consulted the archives of the Devon and Exeter Institution, the Devon Historical Society, and the county libraries. By the end of that time, she'd filled several pages on her tablet with scribbled notes that she was able, at the click of a button, to convert to neat typing. Plus she had a list of websites in her database for rapid retrieval if she needed to consult them once again. Although she wasn't sure she'd need to. It was pretty clear from what she'd found so far: the official story, as recounted to Charlie by Len, was the one all the main records contained. Aubrey had been sent abroad by his parents to make a life for himself in the East Indies. He'd made a fortune. Married and survived a wife, while siring a son. The pair had returned to England on the death of Aubrey's father and his fortune had saved the estate and the village from disaster.

If it wasn't for the other version of the Whitehead history recounted by Len, or if Esther didn't have a suspicious nature, she'd probably have missed the faint signs that not everything was as it might be.

The first hint came when she checked the records of birth in the parish. Harmony Tucker had been recorded as the mother of Aubrey, born in 1814. The space for father's name was left blank. Surely if Harmony and Aubrey Senior were so much in love, she'd have been happy to register their son with his father's name? But on the other hand, maybe Aubrey's parents wouldn't allow that. Would they have had the power to prevent their grandchild claiming his paternity? Quite possibly.

The next clue came from the records of a local building company. There was significant repair work carried out on Whitehead House. And there was a record of the magnificent porch being added. But the dates were all wrong. Aubrey had returned from the East Indies in 1830. Legend had it he'd saved the estate. So why was there no record of any work being carried out until 1880, fifty years after his return and several years after his death?

And finally, she traced the records of the company he was supposed to have founded in the East Indies. The list of shareholders' names included one A. Whitehead Esq. But he was not, as they'd been led to believe, a founding partner. His name was added to the directors' listing several years later. And after just three years, his name disappeared once more. Coincidentally, newspaper archives for that year reported a major theft from the company's headquarters. No names were mentioned, but there was a suggestion it was an inside job. A history of the company published on its centenary in 1920 made reference to the incident as a dark day for the company, but revealed that the culprit had never been identified, nor the money recovered.

"Well, Frisk. That makes interesting reading, doesn't it," Esther said as she closed her tablet and stretched her back to ease the effects of sitting at a keyboard too long. "There's nothing definite in there. But I reckon there could well be something to old Len's gossip." She looked at the clock.

Nearly five. Time to do a bit of work on her latest art commission. But she'd have plenty to tell the others when the Gang of Four got together around the kitchen table in the morning.

CHAPTER 50

"Right, I think that's everything." The year twelve girl with long red hair and a skirt way shorter than school regulations permitted flashed a smile at Rohan and pointed to the table in the window where a group of teenagers was seated. "We'll be over there. Give us a shout when it's ready and we'll come and carry the tray for you."

"She obviously thinks you're too ancient to do it yourself," said Celia with a grin. She opened the glass cabinet and started filling plates with scones and cakes.

"Hey, I'm only thirty-five!"

"Which makes you roughly twice their age, Rohan. And to a teenager, anyone over thirty is well past it."

"Well, she's in for a surprise then, isn't she," Rohan responded tartly as he loaded cups and saucers onto a tray. "I'll take these across first and come back for the rest."

When he reached the table, the girls were all playing with their phones and swapping pictures of dogs on Instagram. At least that's what Rohan assumed they were using. Maybe they'd moved on to another platform by now. He'd have to check with Esther. He felt a warm glow as he thought of his new landlady. He was really looking forward to living on the farm.

"Hey, look, this one's just like Tinker." The girl held out

her phone for Rohan to see. "You're going to be seeing a lot of him, aren't you?"

Good grief, thought Rohan. *News certainly gets around quickly in a village.* But there was no malice in the girl's smile. So he just nodded.

"That's right. And I love dogs. We always had a houseful at home when I was growing up. Haven't been able to have one all the time I've been in digs. So it'll be good to have them around once more."

"Well, you're in the right place if you're a dog lover," said one of the boys. "Coombesford's full of them."

"My favourite's little Benny," piped up one of the others.

"Benny? Which one's that?" It wasn't a name Rohan had come across so far.

"Old Henry Whitehead's little Jack Russell."

"Bertie, not Benny," said someone.

"Yeah, sorry, I meant Bertie. You must have seen him. They're never separated. Never see one without the other."

"Apart from that one time." It was the redhead. "I saw Henry coming out of the church and crossing the green on his own."

Rohan's ears pricked up.

"Really? When was that?"

"Not sure, to be honest. A couple of weeks back, I think." Then she clicked her fingers and pointed to one of her friends. "No, I do remember. It was a Sunday. We'd got a history test the following day and I'd been over at yours to revise. Remember. Something we'd talked about was really bugging me. I stopped to Google it and saw Henry across the road. I was going to call over and ask where Bertie was, if he was okay, but he was gone before I had a chance." She shrugged. "He must have been fine, though, as I saw them walking together the next day."

"I'm just slipping out the back to make a call, Celia," said Rohan. Pulling his phone from his pocket, he hit the first number on his redial list. "Esther, it's me. Can you get hold of Charlie and Annie? We need a meeting, tonight." He

179

paused then went on. "No, I don't think it can wait until tomorrow. And I suspect, when we've talked everything through, we're going to have to disturb DS Smith's evening too."

CHAPTER 51

"Look, Mama C, they are coming out. I can see her." Suzy jumped up from her seat in the front pew and waved her arm over her head. "Hello, Mama Annie!"

"Ssh, Suzy, sit down, they're about to start," hissed Charlie, grabbing her daughter by the arm and pulling her back into her seat. She winked at her partner who was sitting in the front row of the chorus, looking like she was trying not to laugh. Rohan and Esther, sitting beside the excited young girl, exchanged a grin.

The lights went down, and Michael Henning walked up the aisle to enthusiastic applause from the packed audience. He picked up his baton, smiled at the chorus then nodded to the orchestra who began to play the overture.

The Hero's Return had begun.

By the closing notes, two hours later, it was clear that Isabella and Michael had written some beautiful music together. Even Charlie, who hadn't really been looking forward to the evening, had to admit she'd enjoyed it. And not just because of Annie's singing. Edward Jennings, drafted in at the last moment to replace Gavin, had given a stirring performance as the young man torn away from his sweetheart. And Amanda's portrayal of Harmony had brought a tear to many an eye in the church. Melanie had managed her solo beautifully. She'd blushed deep pink when Edward had stood at the end of her aria and whistled loudly.

As the applause died down, Henry Whitehead rose from his seat at the side of the stage and walked to the front. He reached into his pocket and switched on his lapel microphone.

"Ladies and gentlemen. What can I say? Great-great-great-uncle Aubrey would have been so proud of everyone tonight. It is such a fitting…" He broke off as the door to the church was pushed open with a scraping sound. DS Derek Smith and DC Joanne Wellman entered and began walking up the side aisle. Henry went white. Then he cleared his throat and tried to carry on.

"As I was saying, ladies and gentlemen, my dear ancestor, in fact my whole family, are truly honoured by tonight's performance. I'm very grateful to Michael, the orchestra, the soloists, the chorus and of course, poor dear Isabella, who started this whole journey for us." As he spoke, his eyes kept darting towards the two detectives who'd now reached the front of the church and were standing in the shadows outside the vestry door. Finally, it looked as though he couldn't take the tension any longer. "Detectives," he said, turning to them with a tight smile, "I'm sorry you missed the performance, but do you have some news for us?"

DS Smith walked across and stopped in front of him. "Mr Whitehead. We'd like you to come with us. We've some new information we think you can help us with."

"What, now? Can't it wait until tomorrow? We've got a party planned. It's the big night."

The DS shook his head. "No, I'm afraid it can't wait." He nodded to his colleague who walked forward and took Henry by the arm.

"Henry Whitehead, I'm arresting you on suspicion of the murder of Isabella Street and the attempted murder of Melanie Unwin. You do not have…" There was a collective gasp from the audience, and the rest of his words were lost in a rising torrent of sound. Only Charlie, Rohan and Esther from the audience and Annie in the chorus didn't react.

Henry pulled himself up to his full height and opened his mouth to protest. But he was stopped by a bellow from behind him. Edward Jennings strode across the stage and grabbed Henry by the lapels, pulling him from DC Wellman's grasp and shaking him like a puppy with a rag doll.

"It was you! You tried to kill my Melanie. How could you? What'd she ever done to harm you?"

"Edward, don't," called out Melanie, rising to her feet. Rohan jumped forward and pulled Edward away, as Joanne Wellman took hold of Henry once more. But all the fight had gone out of the older man. He looked as if a pin had pricked him.

"It was an accident. I didn't know she'd drink from that bottle. It was meant to be for Michael." The words were said quietly, but Henry forgot his microphone was switched on. His voice echoed around the church and silenced everyone instantly. "Actually, it wouldn't have killed anyone. It was a diluted extract of Fool's Funnel. I just wanted to make him unwell so he'd drop out of the production." Henry sighed and looked at the detectives. "He told me he'd discovered something exciting that would change the course of the story. I thought he'd come up with the truth. That the official version of Aubrey Whitehead's journey and return was not the true one. I thought Michael was going to destroy our family's reputation." He turned towards the singers behind him on the stage. "I'm sorry, Melanie, I wouldn't have hurt you for the world." He shrugged. "And it was all for nothing. The thing Michael had uncovered was quite harmless. In fact, he thought it was something very positive. He told me my fob watch was much older and more valuable than I realised." He smiled wryly. "Of course, I knew that, plus the fact it was stolen. But Michael didn't. He was genuinely pleased for me."

Henry's face changed into a scowl.

"But Isabella was different. She'd told me on the Friday evening she suspected there was something dodgy about where my family's fortune really came from. She was talking about doing some more research. Thought I'd want to know the truth!" He laughed dryly. "Whereas the opposite was true. I already knew the truth and the last thing I wanted was for it to become public. So I went to see her on the Sunday evening. I was in the churchyard when Michael was leaving. I tried to make her stop. Just leave it alone. But once Isabella got an idea into her head, there was no stopping her. 'If my suspicions are correct,' she said, 'we need to get some justice for all the shareholders he robbed' as she put it." Henry stopped and looked at the audience, most of whom were sitting with open mouths, enthralled by the dramatic turn of events. "It would have destroyed my family's good name in this village. I couldn't let that happen, now could I?"

EPILOGUE
FOUR MONTHS LATER

"What a wonderful day." Annie leaned back against Charlie's shoulder as the pair sat on the outside staircase leading up to their lounge. They'd brought their coffees outside to finish them.

"Magic. And our young flower girl did us proud, didn't she? Not to mention her little companion, Bertie." The small black and white dog curled at their feet opened one eye at the sound of his name, but otherwise didn't stir.

"She certainly did. I thought she was going to sleep in that bridesmaid dress. She didn't want to take it off."

"And did you see Rohan and Esther? They spent all evening dancing together."

"I did, Charlie, yes, I did. Tommy Steele whispered to me at one point that the two are still assuring everyone they're just good friends."

"Ha! Good friends? That's one name for it." Charlie sipped her coffee. "I'm not sure they'll be believed any longer – if they were before now. But most importantly, didn't Melanie and Edward look happy?"

"Yes, I'm so glad they worked out their issues in time."

"What was the problem, anyway, Annie? Did you ever find out?"

"Something or nothing really. Just wedding jitters on both their parts. She thought he was getting tired of the countryside and regretted losing his friends in London. And then there was that silly gossip about Isabella and her tenor. As if that was ever credible."

"Well, there was some truth behind it, to be fair. Isabella was carrying on with a tenor, just not the one Melanie assumed." Charlie took another sip of coffee. "And what about Edward? What was his problem?"

"Well, he was worried he was taking Melanie away from her roots and she'd be unhappy. Silly really. But at least they sorted things out in time."

"And I hear they've put in an offer for Whitehead House? So they won't even be moving away from Coombesford. Which is great."

"It certainly is," agreed Annie. "But talking about tenors, wasn't it great seeing young Gavin today?"

"Didn't he look happy? That break in Wales seems to have done him the world of good. He's starting work with a company somewhere up north next month. And taking acting lessons, I understand."

"And judging by the way he was wrapped around that young soprano this evening, we'll be seeing more of him in the village in the future, I suspect."

"Yes. Apparently he told Esther that's what he'd been doing outside the church that night." Charlie didn't have to explain which night she was referring to. "The pair had started to get friendly, but he was having to keep it quiet so he didn't upset Isabella."

Annie nodded and swallowed the last of her coffee.

"Well, I guess we should give Bertie one last run around the field and call it a night. The Falls won't open itself in the morning. And we've a houseful of guests to feed. Although Penny said she'd come in early and give me a hand. She's still off alcohol while she's waiting for her operation, so she was probably the most sober one there today."

She stood up. But Charlie caught her arm and pulled her

back down onto the step.

"Hang on, sweetheart. Before we go in, there's something I want to ask you. All this talk of weddings has given me an idea. Isn't it about time we thought about tying the knot?"

ENJOYED THIS BOOK?

Reviews and recommendations are very important to an author and help contribute to a book's success. If you have enjoyed *Calamity at Coombesford Church* please recommend it to a friend, or better still, buy them a copy for their birthday or Christmas. And please consider posting a review on your preferred review site.

ACKNOWLEDGMENTS

I am once again very grateful for all the support provided by my friends in the thriving community of writers and readers, both in Devon and beyond.

In particular, my thanks go to Carol Amorosi who once more acted as my writing buddy; to my friends in Chudleigh Writers' Circle and Exeter Writers; and to Jane Anderson Brown, Alex Dawson, Clare Lillington, Suzanne McConaghy, Heather Morgan, Richard Morgan, and Michelle Oucharek-Deo, my wonderfully insightful beta readers.

Berni Stevens (bernistevenscoverdesign.com) is responsible, as always, for the beautiful cover and Otis Lea-Weston continues to develop the map of Coombesford. Julia Gibbs (@ProofreadJulia on Twitter) made sure the final text is as error-free as possible. My thanks go to all of them.

I owe a huge debt of gratitude to my sisters, Margaret Andow and Sheila Pearson, for their analytical reading skills and ongoing cheerleading.

Finally my thanks go, as always, to my husband Michael McCormick, my fiercest critic and strongest supporter, who keeps me going, even when I want to give it all up and eat chocolate.

ABOUT THE AUTHOR

Elizabeth Ducie was born and brought up in Birmingham. As a teenager, essays and poetry won her an overseas trip via a newspaper competition. Despite this, she took scientific and business qualifications and spent more than thirty years as a manufacturing consultant, business owner and technical writer before returning to creative writing in 2006. She has written short stories and poetry for competitions – and has had a few wins, several honourable mentions and some shortlisting. She is published in several anthologies.

Under the Chudleigh Phoenix Publications imprint, she has published, in addition to her novels, three collections of short stories and co-authored another two. She also writes non-fiction, including the *Author Business Foundations* series for writers running their own small business. Her debut novel, *Gorgito's Ice Rink*, was runner-up in the 2015 Self-Published Book of the Year awards. The first in the *Jones Sisters* series, *Counterfeit!* came third in the 2015 Literature Works First Page Writing Prize.

Elizabeth is a member of several writers' groups and is particularly proud to be part of the Pickle Jar with Authors in a Pickle.

For more information on Elizabeth, visit her website: www.elizabethducie.co.uk; follow her on Goodreads, Facebook, or Twitter; or watch the trailers for her books on YouTube. To keep up to date with her writing plans, and for a monthly free short story, subscribe to her email list: elizabeth@elizabethducie.co.uk

OTHER BOOKS BY ELIZABETH DUCIE

Coombesford Books
Murder at Mountjoy Manor
Villainy at the Village Store
Coombesford Calendar volume I
Coombesford Calendar volume II

The Jones Sisters series:
Counterfeit!
Deception!
Corruption!

Other fiction:
Gorgito's Ice Rink
Flashing on the Riviera
Parcels in the Rain and Other Writing

Co-written with Sharon Cook:
Life is Not a Trifling Affair
Life is Not a Bed of Roses

Non-fiction:
Sunshine and Sausages

The Author Business Foundations series:
Part 1: Business Start-Up (ebook only)
Part 2: Finance Matters (ebook only)
Part 3: Improving Effectiveness (ebook only)
Parts 1-3 (print only)
Parts 1-3 Workbook (print only)
Part 4: Independent Publishing

Printed in Great Britain
by Amazon